IOWANS CALLED TO VALOR
BY STEVE MEYER

1993 All rights reserved.
This book, or any portion, may not be reproduced without permission.
Published by Meyer Publishing, Garrison, IA.

ISBN No. 0-9630284-2-1

COMMUNITY COLLEGE LRC
MARSHALLTOWN, IOWA 50158

940409

Cover Photo: Bellevue, Iowa, recruits boarding Steamboat to leave for the Civil War in 1861. (Photo Courtesy State Historical Society of Iowa—Iowa City)

DEDICATION

To my three rays of sunshine; Amy, Emily, and Christen.

APPRECIATION

Credits to all who helped in this book could take an entire chapter in itself. Such an undertaking is not completed without considerable consultation and assistance. Among those that were principle assistants are; the State of Iowa Historical Society offices and staff in Iowa City and Des Moines, the Public Libraries and staff in Garrison and Vinton, the Masonic Temple Library and staff in Cedar Rapids, Mary Foust, Michelle Trimble, and numerous others who provided technical assistance in the content and review of this book. Many others helped with bits of wisdom, folklore, and helping me locate resource material. To all I extend my sincere thanks for helping in this adventure.

THE AUTHOR.

TABLE OF CONTENTS

PAGE

INTRODUCTION ...7
THE HAWKEYE STATE'S COMMITTMENT ...9
IOWANS IN THE PRELUDE ...10
LINCOLN'S IOWA TIES ...12
THE CHIEF CONFEDERATE IN IOWA ...14
SOLDIERLY WRITINGS ...15
LOCAL COMPANIES FILL THE FIRST REGIMENTS ...16
EQUIPPING IOWA'S RECRUITS ...20
THE HAWKEYE STATE HELPED FOOT THE BILL ...30
THE CAVALRYMEN ...32
COUNSEL TO VOLUNTEERS ...35
ON THEIR WAY ...36
IN CAMP ...44
MAINTAINING THE SUPPLY OF SOLDIERS ...70
A RECRUITMENT STORY ...79
MARCHING ACROSS IOWA ...82
IOWANS OUT OF THE NORM ...98
ORGANIZATION AND ELECTIONS ...105
INSIGNIA OF RANK IN THE ARMY OF THE UNITED STATES ...109
BACK HOME, ALL WAS NOT WELL ...111
THE FIRST DEATHS ...115
IOWA THREATENED ...121
REFERENCES ...127

INTRODUCTION

The story of Iowans in the Civil War began, as did the Unions, with the Confederate attack on Fort Sumter during the early morning hours of April 12, 1861. Confederate forces lead by the South's first Brigadier General, Piere Gustave-Toutant Beauregard, emerged the victor in that first battle of the war. Two days later came the Presidential proclamation:

Whereas, The laws of the United States have been and now are violently opposed in several States, by combinations too powerful to be suppressed in the ordinary way: I therefore call for the militia of the several States of the Union, to the aggregate number of 75,000, to suppress said combination and execute the laws. I appeal to all loyal citizens to facilitate and aid in this effort to maintain the laws and integrity of the perpetuity of the popular government, and redress wrongs long enough endured. The first service assigned to the forces, probably, will be to repossess the forts, places and property which have been seized from the Union. Let the utmost care be taken consistent with the object, to avoid devastation, destruction, interference with the property of peaceful citizens in any part of the country; and I hereby command persons composing the aforesaid combination to disperse within twenty days from date.

I hereby convene both Houses of Congress for the 4th day of July next, to determine upon measures for public safety which the interest of the subject demands.

ABRAHAM LINCOLN
President of the United States.

Wm. H. Seward, Secretary of State.

Thus, with the call to arms issued, began the most epic debacle of American history. At the time, many speculated it would be a war of only three months. The war of three months did not end until General Robert E. Lee surrendered his Confederate Army to General Ulysis S. Grant at Appomattox, Virginia, on April 9, 1865, and Confederate General Joe Johnston surrendered his Army to General William Tecumseh Sherman the morning of April 17, 1865.

Every Iowan who served in the Civil War experienced four distinct phases in their military career however long or short:
1) Enlisting
2) The camp of instruction
3) War
4) The expiration of their term of service, disability, or death.

In this brief trilogy of Iowa's involvement in the Civil War we peer into events long past connected with the soldier's enlistment, the camp of instruction, and a few other significant bits of trivia concerning Iowa and the Civil War. As much as possible, the actual words the soldiers scribed in letters, diaries, journals, and war accounts are used to divulge events of this period.

THE HAWKEYE STATE'S COMMITTMENT

In all, more than 76,000 Iowa men, nearly one half of all the military age men in Iowa, served in the war between the states. It would seem unlikely that Iowa, one of the most unpopulous states of the Union, and remote from the great battles of the east, would be candidate for the most dedicated state to the cause. Yet, as a state, Iowa in proportion to its population, provided more troops than any other state in the Union. When the data on calls, quotas, credits, and men furnished for the Union armies was compiled, War Department records show that Iowa was called upon for 79,521 troops and furnished 78,095. Sixty-seven men paid commutation, an option that allowed drafted men to buy their way out of military service. Less than 4000 men, including substitutes (an option that allowed a draftee to supply an able bodied man in his place), were drafted in Iowa. Comparing the number of men Iowa furnished with the population of Iowa, which was 674,913 in 1860, the state furnished over ten percent of its population to the war effort. If only those eligible for military service are considered the per cent is increased to over forty three.

By wars end Iowa would muster; 46 infantry regiments, 9 cavalry regiments, and 4 batteries of light artillery, plus thousands of replacement units and 440 soldiers who served in one of the Union's two totally black regiments. Approximately 200 Iowans served in the regular U. S. Army during the war, and some served in the Navy. Iowans also served on the home front in the Northern (320 soldiers) and Southern Brigades (900 soldiers) and the Mississippi Marine Brigade (25 soldiers). Two hundred thirty Iowans served in the Engineer regiment of the west. Additionally, numerous men, particularly those along Iowa's border, joined companies raised in border states. Also, Iowa was at the time a relatively new state just undergoing the settlement process, many who had migrated to Iowa from other states returned to serve in regiments of their their native states. An exact number will probably never be known, but records suggest the number of Iowans who enlisted in regiments of other States to be around 2,000 with nearly half being in the State of Missouri.

One out of five Iowans who enlisted, 13,001, gave the supreme sacrifice for the Union. Of these, 3540 died or were mortally wounded in battle, 515 died as prisoners of war, 448 died of accidents and other causes and 8,498 died of disease. Fewer states suffered proportionately greater losses of their native sons in those four years that tested our nation as it had never before been tested, and has not been tested thereafter.

IOWANS IN THE PRELUDE

Radical abolitionist John Brown can be theorized as being as much a fundamental part of the Civil War as slavery itself. Brown was a wanderer, and a man driven to extremes by his antislavery convictions. Beginning in 1855 he used his family to assist him in his various vendettas aimed at eradicating slavery. In August of 1855 he and five of his sons traveled to Kansas, a state caught in the crossfires of pro-slavery/antislavery sentiment. There he helped the state become a haven for antislavery settlers. As Brown's campaigns against slavery progressed, at least one to the point of murder, he attracted attention and successfully recruited a "company" of followers. Brown's activities culminated with his famous raid on the Harpers Ferry Arsenal in Western Virginia.

Brown had spent some time in Iowa, and had among his followers four men from Iowa; Steward Taylor, Jeremiah G. Anderson, and two brothers—Edwin and Barclay Coppoc. These men became part of Brown's entourage following a brief stay by Brown and his followers in Springdale, Iowa, in 1857 and 1858. All four, being staunch abolitionists themselves, were caught up in Brown's fervor against slavery. They trained with Brown's private militia and followed him, to his final demise.

Edwin (left) and Barclay Coppoc.
(*Photo Courtesy Davenport Academy of Science as printed in the Palmisist of January, 1960. State Historical Society of Iowa*)

Browns demise began in the early morning hours of October 16, when Brown and his 21 member militia successfully captured and held Harpers Ferry for 36 hours. Brown's motive in attempting to capture the arsenal was arms and ammunition. He was sure he could then arm thousands of would be followers. Three members of his company, including Barclay Coppoc, were left behind to guard camp while Brown and his militia embarked on their fateful raid. In Harpers Ferry, citizens and merchants were taken prisoner during the siege. Word of the capture traveled quickly through the surrounding communities. Armed farmers and local militia poured into town and a general battle ensued. Brown with a few members of his company, including Steward Taylor, Jeremiah Anderson and Edwin Coppoc (Edwin Coppoc was designated a lieutenant in Brown's militia), holed up in a fire engine house. During this time Edwin Coppoc shot and killed the Mayor of Harpers Ferry, Fontaine Beckman. The following morning a detail of United States Marines under command of Colonel Robert E. Lee stormed Brown's hold out. Edwin Coppoc at one point in the final hours of the incident had Colonel Lee in the sights of his rifle, but was prevented from shooting by another member of Brown's militia who feared raging retribution from the marines if their commander was killed.

In the final assault on Brown's last stand, Steward Taylor and Jeremiah Anderson were killed and Edwin Coppoc was taken captive along with Brown and others. Brown was hanged on December 2, 1861. Edwin Coppoc was hanged the following day. John Brown handed a final written statement to a guard as he was escorted to the gallows; "I, John Brown am now quite certain that the crimes of this guilty land will never be purged away, but with blood." Barclay Coppoc and four others escaped the fracas at Harpers Ferry. After a long and arduous trip, during which the escapees were highly sought, Barclay made his way back to Iowa. Iowa Governor Samuel J. Kirkwood later refused extradition of Barclay Coppoc to Virginia to stand trial. Following the start of the Civil War, Barclay joined a Kansas Infantry Regiment where he received the commission of Lieutenant on July 24, 1861. He returned to Springdale on a recruiting mission where he recruited eleven young men who had been classmates. Tragically, he was killed on his return trip to Kansas when his train plunged off a bridge over the Platte River that had been partially burned by rebel guerrillas.

LINCOLN'S IOWA TIES

The man who led as no president had before, or has since, and upon whose shoulders rested the sanctity of restoring a "United States Of America," had Iowa ties. Abraham Lincoln's Iowa ties began as a result of his brief military service during the Black Hawk War. In return for his service, he was given three land warrants, two of which he took in Iowa. The first, a forty acre tract fourteen miles northwest of Toledo in Tama County, Lincoln received in 1852. This land was worth $10.00 an acre when he acquired it, and it was sold by his heirs after his death. Lincoln's second military land warrant was a 120 acre tract eight miles northwest of Denison in Crawford County. This parcel was sold by his son Robert Todd Lincoln in 1892 for $1,300. The Denison Daughters of the American Revolution in 1923 erected a boulder and a copper plate on the land as a reminder that it was once owned by Lincoln. In addition to his military land warrants, Lincoln acquired some small lots and parcels of land near Council Bluffs from a Norman B. Judd in 1859. In 1867 Lincoln's heirs reconveyed them back to Mr. Judd.

Other Lincoln Iowa ties occurred during his profession as an attorney. He was prominent as a competent attorney on railroad matters. In September 1857 he tried a case involving the wreck of the steamboat Effie Afton on the Rock Island Bridge in 1856. Lincoln never actually set foot in Iowa during the trial which was held in United States circuit court in Chicago. In the case, he successfully defended the interests of the Rock Island Railroad, establishing the rights of railroad travel on bridges over rivers as commensurate with that of steamboat travel up and down rivers. In another of Lincoln's legal workings with railroads previous to his presidency, Lincoln visited Greenville M. Dodge in Council Bluffs. Dodge was conducting survey work for the Rock Island Railroad at the time. Subsequent to his visit Dodge would become a Major-General in the Union Army, serving with Generals Grant and Sherman. Lincoln remembered Dodge, and during his Presidency called him to Washington D.C. for conferral when congress passed the act providing for a transcontinental railroad. The conference established Council Bluffs as the eastern terminus of the UnionPacific Railroad.

No rendition of Lincoln in Iowa would be complete without mention of his political parlaying in the state. In 1858 during the famous Lincoln-Douglas Debates, Lincoln made a trip across the Mississippi River to Burlington where he delivered a speech at Grimes Hall on October 9th. Clark Dunham, editor of the Burlington Hawk-Eye gave the following comment on Lincoln's oration:

"Grimes Hall was filled to its capacity....So great was the sympathy felt here in the spirited canvass in Illinois, and so high the

opinion entertained of the ability of Mr. Lincoln as a speaker that a very short notice brought together from twelve to fifteen hundred ladies and gentlemen.

High, however, was the public expectation, and much as was anticipated, he, in his address of two hours, fully came up to the standard that had been erected. It was logical discourse, replete with sound arguments, clear, concise and vigorous, earnest, impassioned and eloquent. Those who heard him recognized in him a man fully able to cope with the little giant [Douglas] anywhere, and altogether worthy to succeed him...."

Lincoln was defeated by Douglas in that senatorial race, the greatest blessing of the age. If Lincoln had won our nation would have been without his leadership during our country's most trying hour.

Abraham Lincoln spent no great amount of time in Iowa. In fact, he only made one more Iowa speaking appearance during the summer of 1859 in Council Bluffs before his election to the presidency. Yet, he had the sound support of Iowa. Iowa troops in the Civil War gave him a smashing majority in his election over General McClellan for President in 1864 and the majority of Iowans supported his Presidential election in 1860 and 1864. He remembered some of his Iowa associations when he reached the White House. As President, he appointed James Harlan of Mount Pleasant as Secretary of the Interior and Samuel Freeman Miller of Keokuk to the United States Supreme Court. Lincoln's only surviving son, Robert Todd Lincoln, married James Harlan's daughter. And, a lady named Annie Turner Wittenmyer from Keokuk helped Lincoln lay the foundation for Diet Kitchens that saved many soldiers' lives during the Civil War.

THE CHIEF CONFEDERATE IN IOWA

A little known facet of Confederate President Jefferson Davis' life is that of his stay in and near Iowa during the early years of his military career. Following his graduation from West Point in 1828 Davis joined the First Regiment U.S. Infantry. He was detailed with the 1st to Fort Crawford in Prairie du Chien, Wisconsin and Fort Winnebago a little farther up the Wisconsin River until 1833. During his time in the area Davis made at least two forays into Iowa. In 1831 he superintended construction of a sawmill used to supply lumber for Fort Crawford on the Yellow River in Allamakee County. Davis spent the winter at the mill where he and those in his company built themselves a "rough little fort." He got along so well with native indians that he was adopted into their tribe and given the name Little Chief. His stay at the mill area was not, however, without its hardships. During the winter he caught pneumonia and became so emaciated that his negro slave had to carry him from his bed to a window where he directed mill operations. Davis apparently returned to Fort Crawford for a while, but is shown to have been at the mill again during the fall and winter of 1832-1833 after which he was transferred to the western frontier.

Jefferson Davis' other Iowa adventure was to the lead mining area around Dubuque sometime during 1832-1833. His duties in the area at the time was restoring peace between Indians and other miners in the area. Some dispute had arisen over mining claims which Davis apparently settled by persuading the other miners to leave their claims alone until Iowa became a state.

What effect Davis' stay in and near Iowa had upon the molding of the future President of the Confederacy can only be hypothesized. No doubt the hardships he endured while at what became known as the Jefferson Davis Sawmill influenced the character of a man destined to lead a nation of thirteen seceded states through trials unheard of. And, no doubt his abilities to negotiate the legislature of his country were influenced by skills Davis mastered in hammering out a deal between rival mining factions in the Dubuque area.

SOLDIERLY WRITINGS

The words our Iowa sons wrote during the Civil War provide the greatest revelation of their experiences. Many left diaries, war correspondences, and reminisces for us of later years to ponder in our quests to "feel" the war they fought. From such writings comes indeed the most stoic revelation of Iowa in the Civil War. That writing was a big part of a soldiers daily life is best revealed by one Cyrus F. Boyd of Company G, 15th Iowa Infantry, who recorded the following about his war time writings:

DAILY JOURNAL

This book is compiled from the notes of several small memorandum carried in my pocket which were kept from the date of my enlistment in the Army that was raised to put down the Great Rebellion of 1861.

The design being to keep a record of what was seen and experienced by myself during the trials of those bloody years which followed Very little in this Journal will be known to history as it shall be written here-as one's own providence is quite limited in War, confined to the narrow bounds of a few companions and the little orbit in which he moves, Like a spoke in a great wheel moved by the motion of some great invisible power and not permitted to know why or wherefore he is expected to perform his part in the great work.

This will also aim to record the doings and the fate of many of my companions Having escaped the uncertain fates of War and lived to record my own part in the great struggle is sufficient satisfaction to warrant me in spending the time in consolidating the notes and memoranda which throughout the term of three years and four months was a daily duty I scarcely ever omitted even in the most unfavorable circumstances of making a note of all of interest that occured around me along our tedious and perilous pathway

A note book in my side pocket was like a pocket knife always at command on the march and a larger book in camp or in the baggage was written up at the first opportunity.

LOCAL COMPANIES FILL THE FIRST REGIMENTS

The war began with the South ready and eager, determined and united. The North was surprised, disorganized, bewildered with conflicting opinions, and was aroused only by the clash of arms. To get the war machine going, the Union needed troops. The government turned to the states as the mechanism of supply. At the beginning of the war in April, 1861 there were no military posts, forts, garrisons, not even a single unit of the regular army in Iowa. The nearest arsenal was in St. Louis. The only arms the state possessed were a few thousand antiquated muskets and rifles that had been distributed by act of Congress among several States in proportion to their representation in Congress.

Though the Union had scarcely begun preparing itself, there had been some early inkling that the citizens of the nation, and Iowa, had better prepare. Hence, a feeble preparation began in January, 1861, when Governor Samuel J. Kirkwood was advised to organize the militia. In regard to commissioning officers for the militia he was to "appoint prompt and able men who, tho' they fear God, have no fear of the devil and NO FEAR OF TRAITORS, and who dare to be MEN, despite of party." Able bodied men were urged to enroll themselves in companies, elect officers, and offer their services to the government. Many Iowans enrolled in independent companies organizing in preparation for rumored hostilities. These companies were of local origin, and were formed on the military principle, having military officers, arms, uniforms, and practice in military drill. Although their chief function was probably social in character, they were highly creditable. The Blues, the Guards, or the Rifles (as they were called), fulfilled the purpose of local clubs. They gave balls, held exhibition drills, and on gala days appeared on parade in resplendent uniforms.

As the spring of 1861 drew near and tensions with seceding states of the south, and threats of further secession grew rampant, people became more and more imbued with the possibility of war, and a martial spirit prevailed in the minds of Iowa men. Independent military companies offered services to the government and people everywhere were half consciously making ready for any emergency. It was reported that "merchants, and laboring-men are all busily engaged-working at their respective callings through the day, and drilling in the evening-preparing themselves to enjoy peace, or encounter war." When the war cloud arose, it was these semi-military companies that were first to offer themselves in the service of their country.

Perhaps the most famous independent company in Iowa was the Governor's Greys, from Dubuque, named in honor of Governor Stephen Hempstead. In a letter on January 15, 1861 to Joseph Holt, Secretary of War, Captain F. J. Herron stated that the Greys had passed a resolution

Governor Samuel J. Kirkwood.
(Photo Courtesy State Historical Society of Iowa—Des Moines)

tendering their services to the President during the insurrection of the South. Other companies followed the example, but sent their resolutions to Iowa Governor Samuel J. Kirkwood. Some companies known as Zuaves were organized in Iowa. One, the Burlington Zuaves became Company E of the First Iowa Infantry Regiment and were ordered into quarters on April 20, 1861. "Zuaves" was a name adopted by many local militia in emulation of the famous French Zuave soldiers who were noted for their dash and courage, as well as their brilliantly colored uniforms, which Civil War Zuave Companies also copied.

Olmsted Zuaves. Photo taken in Des Moines, 1860.
(Photo Courtesy State Historical Society of Iowa—Des Moines)

Colonel John Francis Bates
of the 1st Iowa Volunteer Infantry (ca. 1870).
*(Photo Courtesy State Historical
Society of Iowa—Iowa City)*

Local militia did not have to wait long for their call. Four days following the Confederate attack on Fort Sumter, Simon Cameron (Secretary of War) telegraphed these words to Governor Kirkwood: "Call made to you by to night's mail for one regiment of militia for immediate service." Ten companies, or an aggregate of 780 men, to serve for three months, were asked of Iowa under this, President Lincoln's first call for 75,000 state militia from the Union states. As soon as Cameron's dispatch reached Governor Kirkwood he set about the work of organizing Iowa's First Infantry Regiment which served for three months. "The nation is in peril," proclaimed the Governor. "A fearful attempt is being made to overthrow the Constitution and dissever the Union." The Governor announced that Iowa must form a regiment as its contribution to Lincolns first call for troops. The response was overwhelming, ten times the number required volunteered. On April 29 Governor Kirkwood informed the Secretary of War that: "I can raise 10,000 in this state in 20 days." A week later he asked: "How many more regiments will be required from Iowa and for how long? I am overwhelmed with applications." Governor Kirkwood's applictions had for the most part originated from local militia.

Iowa's first Cavalry Regiment was comprised of the following local Cavalry militia as reported in the VINTON EAGLE Newspaper of Thursday June 21, 1861:

IOWA CAVALRY

On the 5th of June the Companies composing a Regiment of Cavalry to be tenuered by the State of Iowa to the Federal Government held a meeting at Ottumwa. Daniel Anderson was Chairman. The names of the Companies are given as follows:

From Lee county, Keokuk Cavalry, Capt. Therrence.
From Clinton county, Hawk-Eye Rangers, Capt. Leffingwell.
From Des Moines Co., Burlington Mounted Rangers, Capt. Chamberlain.

From Monroe county, Monroe Cavalry, Capt. Anderson.
From Hardin county, Hardin Co. Cavalry, Capt. Swan.
From Johnson county, Johnson Co. Cavalry, Capt. Cruer.
From Keokuk county, Keokuk Co. Cavalry, Capt. Price.
From Pottawatomie county, Pottawatomie Co. Cavalry, Capt. Craig.
From Lucas county, Lucas Co. Cavalry, Capt. Henderson.
From Marshall county, Marshall Co. Cavalry, Capt.Thomson.

The following field officers were chosen: For Colonel, FITZ HENRY WARREN; Lieut. Colonel, Charles E. Moss; Major, E. W. Chamberlain.

Brigadier General Fitz Henry Warren. First Colonel of the Iowa 1st Cavalry Regiment.
(Photo Courtesy State Historical Society of Iowa—Iowa City)

Unknown member of 1st Iowa Cavalry Regiment, probably a Zuave.
(Photo Courtesy State Historical Society of Iowa—Des Moines)

Eli Waring from Manchester, a Second Lieutenant of the 1st Iowa Cavalry Company G.
(Photo Courtesy State of Iowa Historical Society—Des Moines)

EQUIPPING IOWA'S RECRUITS

As Iowans rushed to the Union cause, the war machine strained to equip and outfit the state's eager volunteers. States supplied the troops, but the U.S. government supplied arms and equipment, causing tremendous logistical problems. Government and military officials from Iowa were forced to constantly beg and sometimes manufacture by their own means, much of the equipment needed to outfit Iowa's recruits.

The principle means allowing a soldier to be a soldier, arms, proved the most difficult to procure. Delays in getting arms were frequent, and when arms did arrive they were often unsatisfactory and unserviceable. Iowa's gallant First Infantry Regiment, rendezvoused at Keokuk within weeks of the Civil War's outbreak, but lived in daily expectation of their arms. On May 17, 1861 they received word that two thousand arms had been ordered from St. Louis, "escorted by a company from Quincy," to guard them from secessionists. Received in this batch of arms were obsolete muskets that were said to be more dangerous to friend than enemy, kicking a soldier farther than they could shoot. Some German recruits referred to the antiquated arms as KAH-FUSS, or "Cow Foot." "The bayonets don't shine at all," commented the DES MOINES VALLEY WHIG on May 20, 1861, "and we learn that the soldiers don't much affect the old-fashioned smooth bore."

Colonel Samuel R. Curtis took the matter of arms and equipment into his own hands and traveled to Washington D.C. in May, 1861, where he secured an order for 2000 guns, ammunition, and other supplies. In spite of Curtis' attempts the Second, Third, and Fourth infantry regiments still went into rendezvous at Keokuk without arms. The Third regiment left Keokuk without cartridges or cartridge boxes, "Destitute of all equipment but empty muskets and bayonets, and without means of transportation." Not until August 23 were three thousand "Improved

Sebastion L. Blodgett from New London, of the 6th Iowa Infantry Company K.
(Photo Courtesy State Historical Society of Iowa—Iowa City from the Wright Collection)

Muskets" shipped to Iowa troops in Missouri. Minie rifles were to have been furnished, but instead Iowa troops again received remade old smooth bores.

Arming Iowa troops would be a continual challenge throughout the war. Many of the guns received were old flint-lock muskets that had been altered to percussion type. Of all the musketry and rifles troops used, the Enfield Rifle was the most desirable. During the year 1862 Iowa received from the government 1000 .58 caliber Austrian rifles, 2700 .54 caliber Austrian rifles, 10,000 .58 caliber Enfield rifles, 5900 .72 caliber Prussian rifled muskets, 900 .69 caliber Prussian rifled muskets, 600 .69 caliber Springfield muskets, 1000 caliber .71 Garibaldi rifled muskets, 1200 .58 caliber French rifles, 1200 Colt revolvers, and 1200 sabres, with accoutrements for all. Other arms that would be received during the war were Harpers Ferry muskets, Spencer's carbines, Sharp's carbines, Whitworth rifles, Minie rifles and Navy revolvers.

The Sixth Iowa was armed with "miserable Austrian muskets" of which a Dutch member of the regiment stated; "a man might be killed more as twelve times before de tam ding would shoot off." The Seventh Iowa received Springfield rifles and muskets when at Camp Benton in St. Louis. This regiment was also given eight pieces of artillery. Belgian muskets were supplied to the Eighth Infantry while on their way to St. Louis. "Uneven caliber, some crooked barrels, locks out of repair! The boys called them pumpkin slingers and pronounced the crooked barrels adapted to shooting around hills," was the dissatisfaction expressed by troops of the 8th concerning their weapons.

Joseph N. Ballou from Osceola of the 6th Iowa Infantry Company F.
(Photo Courtesy State Historical Society of Iowa—Iowa City From the Wright Collection)

The Eleventh Infantry Regiment had the distinction of being the first regiment completely uniformed, armed and equipped before it left Iowa, but they too were armed with old smooth bore muskets. The Thirteenth and Fourteenth Infantries were likewise not as fortunate, being armed with Belgian smoothbores and old Harpers Ferry flint-locks converted to percussion. The Twenty-second and Twenty-fourth regiments were com-

Officers of the 22nd Iowa Infantry, from upper left clockwise: Lieutenant Colonel Ephraim G. White of Agency City, Captain Lafayette Mullins from Iowa City, Colonel Henry Graham of Iowa City, Major John Henry Gearke of Iowa City.
(Photo Courtesy Historical Society of Iowa—Iowa City)

pelled to drill with wooden rifles and swords of their own manufacture while in camp.

Infantry regiments were not the only units to experience problems with arms. The Second Iowa Cavalry in the beginning of its service was armed with only sabers and pistols. Later the men received more satisfactory arms, Colt's revolving rifles and Sharps carbines. The Fourth Cavalry Regiment, like the Second, was not so fortunate, being mustered in, and under marching orders for Fort Leavenworth, and still without arms in January, 1862. Not until March, 1862, was a mixed batch of weaponry described as follows, added to the heavy dragoon sabers carried by the Fourth Cavalry:

> *About four hundred men were loaded with "Austrian" rifles, a very heavy and clumsy, though rather short, infantry gun, a muzzle-loader, with a ramrod. Half the remainder had "Starr's" revolver, a five shooter, percussion-cap and paper-cartridge pistol, of a bad pattern and poorly made, while all, or nearly all, received a pair of horse-pistols, to be carried in holsters on the pommel of the saddle, the smooth-bore, single-barrelled, muzzle-loader used in the Mexican war.*

These rifles and revolvers never gained favor in the regiment; indeed, it is probable that they did more harm than good, because there was a general want of reliance upon them. The Starr revolver caused more fear in the regiment than it ever did among the enemy. Its shot was very uncertain, its machinary often failed to work, and it had a vicious tendency to go off at a wrong moment. The holster-pistols were better thought of. They were found to be more effective than the revolvers, and far more easily managed than the rifles. Many of them were retained until the Colt's revolvers came, in 1863.

Occasionally, Iowa troops would secure guns from captured prisoners or a captured store of arms. The First Iowa Cavalry at one time captured seventy-three wagons, five hundred horses and mules, eleven hundred rifles and shot guns, one hundred pistols, commissary stores, and ammunition.

Aside from arms, other equipment was correspondingly difficult to obtain in Iowa, particularly in the early months of war. Uniforms worn by the first companies were made by local seamstresses. The first three regiments, when assembled at Keokuk, presented an appearance resembling a "crazyquilt." With the home-made uniforms of the early regiments, there was no continuity. One company was uniformed in navy blue shirt and grey pants, another in grey jacket and black striped pants, while still another had a dark blue coat, with green trimmings, light blue pants and fatigue caps of dark blue. The First and Second Regiments left Keokuk before their uniforms arrived, while the uniforms for the Third Regiment reached Keokuk the night before the men left for Hannibal, Missouri. The Seventh Iowa Infantry left for the front before it received any uniforms or equipment, and the men were forced to use their gray woolen blankets for both raincoats and overcoats. Other and better uniforms were contracted for by the State.

Calvin B. Lake of West Union. Surgeon for the 7th Iowa Infantry.
(Photo Courtesy State Historical Society of Iowa—Des Moines)

Elliot W. Rice of Oskaloosa. Major and later Colonel of the 7th Iowa Infantry. Promoted to Brigadier General in June 1864.
(Photo Courtesy State Historical Society of Iowa—Des Moines)

When the government began issuing uniforms there was often problems in other respects as seen from the following account provided by a member of the Governor's Greys:

"They are admirable fits, all of them, except say eighty or a hundred....A majority of the boys are able to get their pantaloons from the floor by buttoning the waistbands around their necks-others accomplish this desirable result by bringing the waistbands tight up under the arms and rolling them up six or eight inches at the bottom. To be sure this is a little inconvenient in some respects-a fellow has to take off his belts, then his coat, and then ascend one story before he can reach his pockets, and after reaching them they are so deep that one has to take the pants off entirely before he can reach the bottom. Each pocket will hold a shirt, a blanket and even the wearer himself if at any time he finds such a retreat necessary.

And the coats fit beautifully-almost in fact as well as the pants. To be sure half of them are two feet too large around the waist, and almost as much too small around the chest-but then these two drawbacks admirably offset each other. In the cases of fifteen or twenty of them the top of the collar is but a trifle above the small of the wearer's back, and in the cases of about as many more the same article is a few inches above the head of their owners. The same collar also in some cases terminates beneath each ear, and in many others it sweeps away around in a magnificent curve, forming a vast basin whose rim is yards distant from the neck of its possessor. And the sleeves, too, have here and there a fault-some are so tight under the arms that they lift one up as if he were swinging upon a couple of ropes that pass underneath his armpits-others strike bold-

ly out and do not terminate their voluminous course till at a distance of several inches beyond the tips of his fingers, while others conclude their journey after marching an inch or so below the elbows."

There was considerable suffering among the men of early regiments because of their lack of equipment. Great difficulty was encountered in securing even blankets. Many companies did not have enough blankets to go around, and one company of the Second Regiment had "nary blanket." Patriotic citizens donated blankets by the dozen, some of the companies being supplied before they left home for the place of rendezvous. In fact, in October, 1861, Adjutant General Baker published an order requesting all officers who were sending or bringing recruits, to make known to their men the importance of bringing along at least one good blanket, comfort, or quilt, for each volunteer.

Perhaps the one situation which caused the greatest discomfort to soldiers was lack of shoes. At one time only 25 men in Company H, First Infantry, were able to do camp duty for want of shoes. The shoes that were issued were often poor quality. When the Second Regiment received shoes, one man said he "saw several of those men, that same day, with those same shoes on their feet, and holding in their hands the heels, which had already dropped off from them." Many members of the Fourth Regiment were in camp in Council Bluffs without shoes. Poor shoes and scant clothing was a factor in the mortality rate of the Twelfth Regiment. Lack of shoes would be a constant problem throughout the Civil War. Long, hard, marches wore out shoes quickly, and there was little chance of their being repaired or replaced. Many were the tales of tired and bleeding feet and footprints marked by blood. Soldiers sometimes bound pieces of rawhide on their feet. Several of the men of the Sixth Regiment marched with Sherman to Knoxville, barefooted. Gloves and mittens, too, were lacking.

Although clothing was so scarce, some troops would sell their clothing and equipment for whiskey and the like. In December, 1861, the Fifteenth Regiment was drawn up for inspection, and each man required to show all his "plunder" the object being to find out who were the culprits. Finally, the War Department issued an order prohibiting soldiers from selling or giving away clothing, arms, or equipments.

Despite the fact that equipment in general was scarce and difficult to obtain, the baggage wagons of some companies early in the war, were quite large. Before the war was over, however, Iowa troops learned that heavy equipments were more of a hindrance than an aid. The size of equipment trains is suggested by the incident of Confederate forces capturing thirty-five baggage wagons of the Twenty-first Iowa Regiment. Each company of the Eighth Regiment was allowed two six-mule teams with three for regimental headquarters. The Twelfth Regiment was outfitted with "a full supply of camp and garrison equipage, including Sibley tents, heavy mess chests, axes, spades, picks, with kettles and pans innumerable; and an immense wagon train consisting of twelve wagons, each drawn by six mules; two ambulances, each drawn by four horses." In fact, the regiment set out; "with more baggage and a larger train than would have been allowed three years later for the whole 16th Army Corps." These immense trains of baggage were necessitated in part by such things as tents and mess chests which were, at first, in a form which men could not carry. There were company mess chests, containing tin plates, cups, spoons, knives, and forks for sixteen men. Later in the war, contents of the mess chest was divided up into individual mess "kits," each man carrying his own plate cup, knife, and spoon in his haversack with his rations. The first tents used were circular Sibley Tents which resembled a tee-pee, and accommodated sixteen men who slept with their heads toward the outer edge of the tent. There was room in the center for a fire. These tents were too heavy and unwieldy for active service, and soon gave place to small wedge tents which in turn were supplanted by the "Shelter," or "Pup" tent, just large enough for two men, and so arranged that each man could carry half a tent.

William Haddock from Waterloo of the 12th Iowa Infantry, later promoted to Major of the 8th Iowa Cavalry.
(Photo Courtesy State Historical Society of Iowa—Des Moines)

Transportation of troops was another obstacle. Railways of the day offered free transportation to all volunteer troops, but the mileage of Iowa railroads in 1861 was small. Most troops were compelled to march overland, or travel by stage to rendezvous. Some were carried down the

Mississippi River by boats. Scantily clothed, often without tents, and many of them barefooted, the recruits endured many hardships just to get to camp. Captain D.B. Clarke marched his company of recruits across the state in the cold of December, 1861, from Council Bluffs to Keokuk, with only blankets to supply them.

In the first months tents were used in camp, yet many of the companies lacked them, and they could not be secured from Washington. Orders were given to get tents wherever they could be found. Barracks were provided for later companies. Very rough structures, the lumber was furnished by the government, and the actual work of construction was often done by troops themselves. Some of the barracks were built of pine lumber, others of logs. Some were shingled, while others were not; and some were heated, although most of them were not. In camp one company was assigned to each barrack. The interior of each barrack was built with two platforms, one above the other, each about twelve feet wide, extending the whole length of the building. Each platform was intended to give sleeping accommodations for fifty men, twenty-five on each side, heads together in the middle.

The situation with regard to the rations was no different than anything else. Undoubtedly many of the companies received sufficient food over considerable periods of time, but many did not. The first companies, while in rendezvous camps, were regaled with every kind of gustatory luxury, often provided by locals. Later, it was hard tack, salt pork, and what ever else could be procured, often by indiscriminate means. The one item there seems to have been no lack of among early regiments is beer and other liquors which were supplied by friendly citizens in great quantities.

One item of pride for every regiment and/or company was its flag. Each was distinct and the gift of home communities, very often the handiwork of local women. Sometimes complimentary equipment and regimental provisions were also presented to the officers.

Some States seemed to receive better treatment from the U.S. Government in securing equipment than did Iowa. It seems Iowa was often ignored or given left over old junk refused by eastern troops. A member of the Seventh Iowa Infantry wrote home from Bird's Point in the fall of 1861 that "it makes quite a difference whether a regiment hails from Iowa or from Illinois. Should strap officials recognize the difference between Hawkeyes and Suckers. It has been with difficulty that our claims at the Quartermasters and pay department could be recognized until Illinois regiments had been attended to first." And a letter from a soldier of the first Iowa appearing in the May 17, 1863 DUBUQUE HERALD expressed: "Why is it our Iowa regiments cannot be armed and equipped, say one-half as well as the regiments of Illinois? All of the latter are armed with the very best arms in use, either Sharpe's or Minie rifles—our men are put off with an old rusty machine that is a cross between a blunderbuss and a Chinese matchlock, and is one which would excite the merriment even of a Digger Indian, unless he happened to be behind it."

Only by persistent efforts of Governor Kirkwood and the states military commanders did Iowa troops ever receive suitable arms and equipment. Their efforts produced some breaks in the record of delay and disregard. Members of the Nineteenth Regiment, when they left the State for St. Louis, were in possession of "superb equipments". The Twenty-second Iowa and the Thirtieth Iowa were speedily equipped upon their mobilization. The Forty-second Regiment received "overcoats, underclothes, hats, feathers, shoes, bugles, small drums and other trimmings" before leaving Dubuque. At one time, men of the Thirty-fourth Regiment were in such good condition and so well equipped that in a prize drill with five of the best companies in the division, this regiment was the star. The Twelfth Iowa Infantry owing to persistent efforts by their Colonel Woods received the very best, Enfield rifles, so also did the Twenty-first, Twenty-fourth and the Twenty-fifth infantry regiments.

John C. Schader from Shueyville. Surgeon of the 22nd Iowa Infantry.
(Photo Courtesy State Historical Society of Iowa—Iowa City)

Jacob H. Fleagle from Mount Pleasant, of the 25th Iowa Infantry Company B. Fleagle died of disease on Nov. 19, 1862 at Helena, Arkansas.
(Photo Courtesy State Historical Society of Iowa—Des Moines)

Some cavalry regiments were very well equipped. The big task of outfitting cavalry was securing acceptable horses. Cavalry horses were required to be fifteen hands and one inch high, and from five to nine years old. To some companies horses were furnished by the government.

Soldiers who owned their own horses were paid forty cents per day for the use of their mounts. Horses, arms, and accoutrements of the First Iowa Cavalry Regiment were said to be excellent. The Third Cavalry was speedily equipped and reported in December of 1861 to be fully armed and equipped with carbines, sabres, and navy revolvers. The Second Iowa Cavalry, after it was transformed, in March, 1864, into the Second Iowa Cavalry Veteran Volunteers, was, on the 19th of June, "armed with Spencer's Seven Shooting Carbines." This was the best arm in service at the time, and could shoot fourteen balls per minute. Some Confederate prisoners captured by the Second Cavalry, "asked to see one of the guns you all fight with," and added, "you bring them to your shoulder and hold them there, while a continuous stream of lead rolls from them into our faces. It is no use for us to fight you'ens with that kind of gun." Another prisoner said of the Spencer's Carbines; "loaded Sundays and fired all the week."

THE HAWKEYE STATE HELPED FOOT THE BILL

All expenses of volunteer troops were paid by the State of Iowa from the time they were ordered into quarters until they were mustered into the United States service. In May of 1861 the General assembly authorized issuance of bonds to the amount of $800,000, and use of State funds for expenses of enlistment. To solve the fiscal problems created for Iowa by the war effort, everyone pitched in. Solomon Sturges, a Chicago millionaire offered to loan Governor Kirkwood $100,000. The banks of the State, namely the State Bank and its branches, rallied in support of the Governor. Town funds were made up, at Brighton $1250 cash was raised in a few minutes from Republicans and Democrats alike, and much more was promised to help feed and clothe Iowa Troops. Many locally prominent individuals were active in raising funds to equip Iowa's troops. No doubt scores of long forgotten community fund raisers were the backbone of funding expenses, such as those incurred by the state in mustering the First Iowa Infantry Regiment as reported in the June 20, 1861 VINTON EAGLE Newspaper:

EXPENSES OF THE FIRST IOWA REGIMENT.

The following items of expenditures were sent to the Legislature by Governor Kirkwood, in obedience to a resolution of that body inquiring into the expenses incurred by the First Iowa Regiment up to the time they were mustered into service at Keokuk:

Uniforms for two Dubuque companies	$1,949.04
Uniforms for one Davenport company	1,100.00
Transportation Dubuque Co. to Davenport	886.00
Subsistence of 3 co's at Dav, to May	1,410.00
Transporting three companies to Keokuk	776.40
Uniforms of Iowa City company	1,150.00
Transporting same to Keokuk	125.00
Iowa City company subsistence	262.50
Uniforms of Cedar Rapids company	1,400.00
Transporting to Keokuk of 3 companies	430.00
Subsistence of Cedar Rapids company	550.00
Muscatine's Uniforms and subsistence	2,000.00
Uniforms of 2 Burlington & 1 Mt Pleasant Co	3,000.00
Transportation and subsistence of same	1,619.58

Subsistence to May 4th	2,200.00
Tents, blankets, &c., &c.,	8,331.30
Total	$27,229.89
Estimated pay of officers and men while under service of the State	$12,000.00
Grand total cost of First Regiment	$39,229.89

THE CAVALRYMEN

No soldier presented a more formidable sight than the mounted cavalry soldier with all of his arms and acoutrements. Following is a graphic description taken from Scott's "The Story of a Cavalry Regiment: The Career of the Fourth Iowa Veteran Volunteers:"

Mounted upon his charger, in the midst of all the paraphernalia and adornments of war, a moving arsenal and military depot, he must have struck surprise, if not terror, into the minds of his enemies. Strapped and strung over his clothes, he carried a big sabre and metal scabbard four feet long, an Austrian rifle or a heavy revolver, a box of cartridges, a box of percussion caps, a tin canteen for water, a haversack containing rations, a tin coffee-cup, and such other devices and traps as were recommended to his fancy as useful or beautiful. The weight of all this easily reached or exceeded twenty-five pounds. The army clothing was heavy, and, with the overcoat, must have been twenty pounds. So this man, intended especially for light and active service, carried on his body, in the early part of his career, a weight of nearly fifty pounds. When he was on foot he moved with a great clapping and clanking of his arms and accoutrements, and so constrained by the many bands crossing his body that any rapid motion was absurdly impossible. When he was mounted, his surrounding equipments were doubled in number and his appearance became more ridiculous. His horse carried, fastened to the saddle, a pair of thick leather holsters with pistols, a pair of saddle-bags filled with the rider's extra clothing, toilet articles, and small belongings, a nose-bag, perhaps filled with corn, a heavy leather halter, an iron picket-pin with a long lariat or rope for tethering the horse, usually two horse-shoes with extra nails, a currycomb and horse brush, a set of gun-tools and materials for the care of arms, a rubber blanket or poncho, a pair of woolen blankets, a blouse, a cap or hat, and such other utensils and articles of clothing or decorations the owner was pleased to keep. This mass of furniture, with the saddle, would weigh in most cases seventy pounds. So, in the first marches, the unfortunate horse was compelled to carry a burden ranging from two hundred to two hundred and fifty pounds. When the rider was in the saddle, begirt with all his magazine, it was easy to imagine him protected from any ordinary assault. His properties rose before and behind him like fortifica-

tions, and those strung over his shoulders covered well his flanks. To the uninitiated it was mystery how the rider got into the saddle; how he could rise to a sufficient height and how then descend upon the seat was the problem. The irreverent infantry said it was done with the aid of a derrick, or by first climbing to the top of a high fence or the fork of a tree.

It was perhaps due to the custom of carrying these complex incumbrances that the story became current among the rebels in the East, in the early part of the war, that the Yankee cavalrymen were strapped to their saddles to prevent their running away.

Yet some of the men were not content with the regulation load. They added a set of plate-armor to it. Among the scores of articles for various uses which were peddled in the camps within the first year of the war, was an "armored vest." It was a vest of blue cloth, cut in military style, with two plates of steel, formed to fit the body and fastened between the cloth and the lining, so as to cover the front of the wearer from the neck to the waist. Samples of the plates were exhibited in the camps, with deep marks upon them where bullets had failed to penetrate a spectacle which, with the glib tongues of the dealers, induced a few of the officers and men to buy; and some of the horses, acordingly, had eight or ten pounds more to carry.

Not for long however, did any of the horses bear these dreadful loads. The evident bad effect upon the horses, the care of so many articles, the fact that some of them were not used often enough to justify the trouble of keeping them, and the invaluable lesson steadily taught by experience, that only a few things are really needed by a soldier, presented a succession of reasons for diminishing the inventory. The few "armored vests" disappeared on the first march. The lariat was of little use, it often entangled the feet of horses and burned them, and, with its big picket-pin, it was "lost". The nose-bag was thrown away by many, and carried empty as much as possible by others. The riders clothing was reduced to the least possible-a mere change of underclothing in addition to the garments worn. The hat was stripped of its trimmings, or disappeared entirely in favor of the cap. The pair of blankets was reduced to a single one. Of the small articles for toilet and other uses, only those absolutely necessary were retained. One horseshoe and four nails only were carried, unless there was an express order to carry more. If a curry-comb or brush disappeared, no matter, -one man with a *comb and another with a brush had enough for two. Even the supply remaining according to this description was further reduced by many of the men. It became a fine art how to lessen the burden of the horse; and the best soldiers were those whose horses were packed so lightly that the carbine was the biggest part of the load. If it is a wonder in the first campaign how a cavalryman could get on to or move his horse when equipped for the field, the wonder afterwards came to be, how a man could live with so meagre an equipment.*

Unidentified member of the 5th Iowa Cavalry.
(Photo Courtesy State Historical Society of Iowa—Des Moines)

COUNSEL TO VOLUNTEERS.

1. Remember that in a campaign more men die from sickness than by bullet.

2. Line your blanket with one thickness of brown drilling. This adds four ounces in weight and doubles the warmth.

3. Buy a small India rubber blanket (only $1.50) to lay on the ground or to throw over you during a rain storm. Most of the eastern troops are provided with these. Straw to lie on is not always to be had.

4. The best military hat in use is the light colored soft felt; the crown being sufficiently high to allow space for air over the brain. You can fasten it up in fair wether or turn it down when it is wet or very sunny.

5. Let your beard grow so as to protect the throat and lungs.

6. Keep your entire person clean: this prevents fevers and bowel complaints in warm climates. Wash your body each day if possible. Avoid strong coffee and oily meat. General Scott said that too free use of these (together with neglect in keeping the skin clean) cost many a soldier his life in Mexico.

7. A sudden check of perspiration by chilly or night air often causes fever and death. When thus exposed, do not forget your blanket.

"AN OLD SOLDIER."

The above advice appeared in the Oct. 23, 1861 issue of the VINTON EAGLE Newspaper. How well the advice was heeded by the thousands of Iowans in camp and in preparation for the war is left to time.

ON THEIR WAY

Iowans became soldiers one of three ways, they enlisted individually, they went in with one of the "Home Guard" units or a locally raised company, or in remote cases they were drafted. In writing their experiences previous to what contemporary military lingo refers to as "boot camp," we see all of the pomp and circumstance surrounding patriotic pep rallies ushering soldiers off to their destinations in camp. Elections of company officers were held, gala community affairs surrounded their embarkation, and the troops at this time seemed somewhat reticent to what actually lay ahead. They were, it seems, gullibly swept up in the aura of patriotism surrounding the Union war machines need for its basic machinery–soldiers.

Alexander Simplot drawing from the May 25, 1861 issue of HARPERS WEEKLY. "Departure of Volunteers From Dubuque"

* * * * *

ERASTUS B. SOPER
12TH IOWA INFANTRY COMPANY D

Excerpts of memoirs written by a man who at the time of his enlistment was a banker and lawyer in Emmetsburg, Iowa. Soper based his memoirs on some of his own war time writings, plus those of Byron Plympton Zuver of Mason City and Edwin A. Buttolph of Cedar Rapids. Soper was one of the many who re-enlisted after having served in the notable First Iowa Infantry. He re-enlisted as Second Sergeant:

This company was recruited at Cedar Rapids, Iowa, between September 20th and October 15th, 1861.

It was composed almost entirely of young men ranging from sixteen to twenty-five years of age. Of the ninety-eight men of which the Company consisted, when mustered in, only five or six were married at the time of their enlistment; and nearly all had been reared on farms. Iowa was then a frontier State. All were pioneers, the sons of the early settlers, enured to the privations incident to pioneer life, and full of the vigor and push of the West; combined with this was the lofty spirit of patriotism, and the hatred of slavery and border ruffianism, born of moral instincts, and strengthened and intensified by the outrages perpetrated by the propagators of slavery during the Kansas-Nebraska troubles. A number of them had dropped everything, and had enlisted in Co. "K" of the 1st Regiment Iowa Infantry in response to President Lincoln's first call for 75,000 men, and had hastened to the front and valiantly served their country more than the stipulated time, and returning to their homes had been received as heroes....

Thomas Z. Cook and John H. Stibbs, who had been respectively the Captain and Orderly Sergeant of Company "K," 1st Iowa Infantry, on September 20th, 1861, set about recruiting a Company to be known as Company "K" 1st Iowa Infantry, should the Regiment be organized; otherwise to go into the 12th Iowa, then about to be organized at Dubuque....Every recruit became a recruiting agent, and with characteristic energy Stibbs prosecuted the work of enrolling the Company. Neighboring settlements were visited, meetings were held in school houses, and recruits secured. Cedar Rapids ...was canvassed, and no young man who could pass muster refused a place. Irish, Bohemian, German and American were alike welcome. By October 10th, about seventy men were enrolled. About this time Robert W. Hilton had about twenty men enrolled at Shellsburg, Benton County, Iowa,....

On the 12th of October, 1861, the recruits having been gathered together at Cedar Rapids, met pursuant to appointment in Carpenters Hall, situated in a Block afterwards transformed into the American House, the corner of 1st Street and 2nd Avenue, for the election of officers. John H. Stibbs was elected Captain, and Jason D. Ferguson 1st Lieut. unanimously, and Hiel Hale on the 1st ballot was elected 2nd Lieut. over Robert W. Hilton. Captain Stibbs, thereupon, appointed Hilton Orderly Sergeant, and announced that he would appoint the other non-commissioned officers at a later day....

On Monday evening October 14th, a banquet was tendered to the departing Company by the ladies of Cedar Rapids.... The boys made their first charge; they captured the table, ate all they could, and in order to settle the matter danced until morning. There may have been sad hearts but they did not so appear. In the small hours of the morning the dancing ceased, and the boys sought a few moments sleep before their departure....

* * * * *

BENJAMIN F. THOMAS
14TH IOWA INFANTRY COMPANY G

The recollections of a young lad from Wolf Creek, a settlement in Northern Tama County:

Oct 27, 1861 We remained at home till the twenty-second day of October when we went to Toledo to join the company. A number of our Buckingham friends went with us that far. When we arrived at Toledo the streets were full of people and they cheered us lustily and shook hands with us vigorously. After a time the company was formed in line and marched to what was then the new Baptist church, where the ladies of Toledo had spread for us and our friends a bountiful dinner....

From Toledo we went in lumberwagons to Marengo, which was the nearest railroad station. The first night we stopped at Irving.

This was the home of a number of our boys. There were about fifty of us all told, and we were distributed among the citizens for lodging.

Had breakfast at half past four and at daylight were off for Marengo, where we arrived about eleven o'clock the same morning. There was much enthusiasm manifested here as there was wherever we went....

Finally we arrived at Davenport. Cheering, cheering cheering on every side. Two other companies who came from the western part of the State were on the train with us. We were all dismounted from the cars and formed into line, and, headed by a brass band, marched out to Camp McClellan....

* * * * *

THE PIONEER GREYS OF CEDAR FALLS

On Saturday night, April 21, 1861, Captain John B. Smith called the Cedar Falls militia company to attention at precisely eight o'clock. As the orderly sergeant clipped through the roll, Smith listened to the staccato responses of sixty of the eighty-two members on the roster of the Pioneer Greys. A strange tenseness prevailed over the company facing their captain in the improvised armory in Overman Hall. War loomed ominously near. Both the captain and the Greys knew that within the hour they would vote for or against offering their services in defense of the Union. As he stood before the Pioneer Greys on that fateful Saturday evening, Captain Smith held in his hand three documents.

First he read aloud President Lincoln's proclamation calling for 75,000 volunteers to suppress the rebellion. Next, he read the second proclamation which had been issued by Governor Kirkwood on April 18, 1861, calling for a response from the citizens of Iowa to fulfill the Presidents request.

After reading these appeals for enlistment, Captain Smith, with a few terse remarks, laid the call to arms before the company. One after another expressed his opinion, leaving no doubt about the ultimate decision. The internal conflict of the men was no doubt intense. Many of the Greys were young married men just beginning to make headway on farms, trades, or professions. To enlist was to subordinate their allegiance to family and business for the welfare of the nation. At last Captain Smith called for the question of volunteering. The vote stood fifty seven in favor and three against. Tremendous applause shook Overman Hall, but Captain Smith checked the cheering of the men while he read an order from Jesse Bowen, the Adjutant General of Iowa. Apparently Bowen entertained no doubt that the Pioneer Greys would offer their services, for he directed Captain Smith to bring his company up to war-time strength and have it prepared for rendezvous by May 20th.

According to the official regulations issued by the Adjutant General of the United States on May 4, 1861, each company in the Union Army would consist of a captain, a first lieutenant, a second lieutenant, a first sergeant, four other sergeants, eight corporals, two musicians, and not less than sixty-four or more than eighty-two privates. Of the eighty two men on the roster of the Pioneer Greys, some had physical conditions and others had obligations which prevented their enlistment. Captain Smith hoped to raise the strength of the company as fas as possible beyond the seventy-five required minimum. Two energetic young men were dispatched to recruit as many men as possible from Cedar Falls, Waverly, Charles City and neighboring communities. Three days later they arrived back in Cedar Falls with an additional fifteen recruits and proudly reported that within a few days twenty-five more would arrive from the "up country." The new recruits and the Greys promptly marched through the streets in a procession headed by the Cedar Falls Brass Band playing a number of patriotic songs. A cheering crowd of hundreds gave them a rousing pep rally.

On May 17th Governor Kirkwood received a request from the War Department for more troops. The Governor immediately ordered the Second and Third Iowa regiments to renezvous at Keokuk on May 25th and June 3rd respectively. The Pioneer Greys were placed in the Third Regiment of Iowa Volunteer Infantry as Company K. Their term of service would be for three years, or the duration of the war if it be shorter than three years. More recruits continued to swell the ranks of the Greys, and in the final week the Greys were in Cedar Falls, Captain Smith inaugerated intensive military training for the company. He required the men to report daily for drill at nine in the morning, four in the afternoon and again in the evening.

On Sunday morning May 26th as Cedar Falls citizens were on their way to church, they learned that Captain Smith had received the official summons calling for the Greys to report for active military duty. The news circulated rapidly that they must be ready in a few days. The Greys would travel via rail car to Dubuque where they would board a steamboat to Keokuk for intensive military training.

As preparations were made for the embarkation of the Greys, the entire community helped. Citizens of Cedar Falls demonstrated that they "stood ready to meet the great struggle for Union, Law, and Freedom." It seemed no one could do too much for the Greys. People dug into their pockets, contributing liberally to such things as soldier relief funds to help the families the departing men would leave behind.

The night of May 27 preparations for the Greys departure came to a head with a community mass meeting held at Overman Hall. Patriotic oratories from prominent citizens and politicians ensued. None of the Greys yet had uniforms, and the government's war machinery was not yet proven capable of providing any on the short notices within which the early regiments were mustered. At the prodding of one speaker a suggestion was made that the citizens send their company off properly attired. The suggestion was received with enthusiasic applause by the crowd. Generous donations from local merchants and wealthy citizens were immediately received for the uniforms.

From Wednesday afternoon, May 29 until Saturday night of that week sixty sewing machines operated by volunteers transformed bolts of grey wool and blue cotton cloth into uniforms for the Greys. Three local tailors volunteered their services and equipment, and assumed the prerogative of "bossing the ladies" in the manufacture. The first uniforms of the Greys, as were many others of local companies, were grey, not "Yankee Blue." Not until the first battles of the war when both Union and Confedearate soldiers clashed, both clad in gray, was it seen that a difference in uniform color was necessary.

For several hours on Sunday morning June 2nd, Overman Hall resounded to the thud of marching feet. Captain Smith had found it necessary to lengthen the drill periods in order to teach the recruits the fundamental military manuevers. Given the stress of the emergency, no one questioned the Captain's requirement of such drilling on holy day. At noon, the Captain snapped "Company Dismissed!" and a special committee went about the work of transforming Overman Hall into an auditoreum that would be fitting for the soldiers' farewell service beginning there at two-thirty. Places to hitch a horse and buggy were a premium for the event, as the citizens of Cedar Falls and surrounding communities turned out in colors. Ministers were on hand to give oratory and to issue their blessing upon the troops, once again persons of local prominence and political office delivered oratories, but this was not enough. It was deemed that on the night of June 3rd, the night previous to the soldiers' scheduled departure, a gala ball should be given for the company in order that the soldiers would have a fitting departure.

Emotions were at a peak as citizens once again gathered on the evening of the third. Renditions were once again heard from the great orators as before, but on this occassion with an even higher tincture of patriotic and emotional verbiage. As a departure gift from the same citizens who had rendered their whole hearted support to the Greys, the First Lieutenant of the company was presented with a Colt Navy revolver and it was announced that a sword and epaulettes had been ordered for Captain Smith. The frivolities which followed during the gala activities of the evening can only be surmised as citizens, soldiers and families all enjoyed one last evening of mutual "company" before the next day's departure.

Five thousand people gathered the next day to see the Greys embark. No occassion in the history of Cedar Falls had yet drawn such crowds. As they prepared to board the waiting train, relatives and friends crowded close around the soldiers for parting words. One hysterical, sobbing, woman with two little children clinging to her skirts begged her husband to stay. So intense was her grief that three young men standing near by offered to take her husbands place. He was, however, determined to go, and go he did.

George D. Perkins, Editor of the GAZETTE watched the proceedings of the departure from the windows of his editorial abode a short distance away. In Friday's GAZETTE, Perkins said of the departure:

> "Mingling hither and thither among the mass could be seen the Greys bidding their friends farewell...Words were few but actions told the feelings of the heart more plainly than they. Stout men would grasp each other by the hand, and while they would not trust themselves to speak the thoughts that came rushing thick and fast, the eyes would suffuse with tears, tears that were no disgrace to manhood. Fathers were parting with children; husbands with wives and brother with sisters....At last came the order for the Greys to fall in; the father snatched the last kiss from his wife and little ones, whose love grasp upon him had to be rudely severed; and parents had to speak the last words of counsel and advice it might be their privelege to offer. But though love of kindred, friends and home were strong, yet duty was paramount to all these, and the Greys promptly obeyed its call."

At nine-thirty the Conductor shouted "All aboard!" After boarding, the engineer backed the train a good distance down the tracks and then brought the train at full steam past the crowded station platform. Such a shout was given by the departing soldiers and spectators as the train passed, that there was little doubt of Cedar Falls' conviction to the cause its sons were embarking upon. As the train passed down the rails, the crowd watched in silence as its first contribution to the war effort disappeared among the oaks lining the Cedar River.

For what was now Company K of the Third Iowa Infantry, their battle with those not on the side of the Union began in just a few days. On Thursday evening, June 6th as Company K awaited the embarkation of the KEY CITY to take it to the rendezvous of the Third Iowa at Keokuk, a man on the wharf audaciously hurrahed for seccession. A soldier from the boat flung a pail at the Copperhead, who just as quickly flung the pail back. The missile struck Lieutenant Fitzroy Sessions of Cedar Falls squarely in the chest, igniting his Scoth-Irish temper. Though the boat was actually pulling away from the wharf, Sessions placed his bowie knife between his teeth, grasped the Colt revolver given to him by the citizens of Cedar Falls, and jumped ashore. With one well placed blow he knocked the Copperhead back about a rod, then turned and leaped dexteriously several feet through the air, back onto the boat.

IN CAMP

Following all the emotions and glowing farewells surrounding a soldiers departure, one step separated them from war– Camp. In camp, rookie soldiers were bugled out of bed at 5 A.M. and prodded through calisthenics on empty stomachs. Then came endless hours of company drills with time out only for meals and maintenance duties of the camp such as hauling water or chopping wood. The illiteracy and uneducated status of those who enlisted at the time is evident in the problems drill instructors (the most unpopular men in Camp) had in teaching men to march. Many recruits had to first learn the difference between their left and right foot! After learning simple marching steps, soldiers graduated to learning tactical maneuvers. Then there were lessons in self defense with bayonet practice, and of course the use of firearms. Loading and firing musket rifles of the age was a nine step process requiring both hands and a good set of teeth. Many were embarrassed in this process the first time when they forgot to remove their ramrod from the barrel, causing them to search through weeds and brush for the vital tool. After camp, most Iowa regiments were shipped to Benton Barracks, or "Camp Benton" as some called it, in St. Louis. Camp Benton was their last stop before going to the front. Not all was work or drudgery in camp, there were moments of gaiety and the usual boyish chivalry that occur when hundreds of men gather in one place.

Iowa regiments rendezvoused, and troops received their initial training at camps all over the state. Four camps were established in Keokuk during the war; Camps Ellsworth, Rankin, Halleck and Lincoln. In Davenport there were five camps; Halleck, Roberts (later Kinsman), McClellan, Joe Holt, and Herron. Dubuque hosted Camp Union (later Camp Franklin), Iowa City: Camps Fremont and Pope, and in Mt. Pleasant was Camp Harlan which later became Camp McKean. Council Bluffs and Clinton both hosted a Camp Kirkwood in honor of Iowa's war governor, and later Council Bluffs hosted Camp Dodge. There was also Camp Warren and Camp Laumen in Burlington, Camp Burnside in Des Moines, Camp Strong in Muscatine and Camp Tuttle in Oskaloosa. Camp Ellsworth in Keokuk was the first Civil War camp established in Iowa in May, 1861. The first arriving troops of the First Iowa Infantry were issued one blanket and a few pieces of mess gear tossed from the back of a quartermaster wagon. "We have plenty of food here," a Fairfield private from the First Infantry wrote to his parents in June, "most of which is beans." He also reported that fifteen members of Company E had worn out their shoes and were barefooted.

1861 Drawing of Camp Kirkwood in Council Bluffs, camp of the 4th Iowa Infantry.
(Photo Courtesy State Historical Society of Iowa—Des Moines)

"Camp Warren-Rendezvous for Iowa Troops." Alexander Simplot sketch in HARPERS WEEKLY, August 24, 1861.

Whether reported fondly or with remorse, every soldier had something to write or recall about their first taste of military life, "In Camp." For many, camp would be the first excursion of their life into the world beyond security of home and family.

* * * * *

FRANC B. WILKIE
WAR CORRESPONDENT

Wilkie was in a different position than the soldier, he went along to observe. Writing for the DUBUQUE HERALD and the CHICAGO TIMES, he carried out the important task of reporting to waiting hearts, what was happening in the lives of Iowa's Boys in Blue. He was there with the First Iowa Infantry at Camp Ellsworth in Keokuk where on June 2, 1861 he reported:

> *The details, both regular and irregular in camp life are varied, and to most of us, amusing and full of interest, all of which will probably wear off after a week's familiarity with its duties. Incessant drilling, guard mounting, either beneath a boiling sun or in a drenching rain storm, sleeping seven in a tent, washing greasy dishes, scouring rusty knives and forks, the almost State's-prison-like confinement of the soldiers; all these, and a hundred other circumstances incident to camp life, will very speedily take the romance out of the whole matter...Theoretically camp life is desirable as a first class situation in Paradise or in the innermost heart of a pretty woman; practically—well "I'd rather be a dog and bay at the Moon" than be a soldier liable to camp duty.*

Wilkie reported that daily camp life consisted of a "Drummers Call" at 4:30 AM when the Drum Band assembled in front of sleeping soldiers' tents. "Reveille" was fifteen minutes later, after which the band marched up and down the length of the soldiers tents and played a half a dozen tunes. At 6:00 AM was "Police Call" when every scrap of paper, bit of straw and refuse was picked up from the camp ground. At 6:30 AM those who were ill reported for "Surgeons Call." Breakfast was at 7:00 AM and at 7:30 drill began. The soldiers ate dinner at noon, at 4:00 PM participated in company parade and at 6:00 dress parade for all the companies. At 9:00 "Tattoo" was sounded by the band playing several musical selections and "Taps" at 9:30 meant lights out in all privates' tents. Captains were allowed to keep their lights on until 11:00 PM.

Some companies, in such humor as only occurs when hundreds of men gathered for weeks on end, kept camp life interesting as Wilkie reported during his stay in camp with the First Iowa:

> About the only object of interest in the streets now is the drill of the Davenport City Guards—Capt. Bob Littlers somewhat famous company of fireman and raftsman. They reminded me very much of the Fire Zuaves of Washington. Their dress is black pants with a greyish stripe, grey shirts, and a grey fatigue cap. One of their amusements is to come up from supper, break into a double quick march, and continue it for a length of time that would tire an ordinary walker. Last night they ran without stopping over four miles, and upon reaching their quarters, instead of "laying up", they "broke out" in a gymnastic sport, greatly to the wonderment of spindle shanked clerks and narrow breasted spectators....In running they go by company front, in single or double files, by platoons or sections, wheel flank, oblique, and thus perform all the evolutions without slackening their pace, and in just as good order as though in the ordinary step. Independent of all these immense physical advantages, the Guards have other features of value—they are sober, gentlemanly, quiet, and are fast getting to be the lions of the town.

The boredom of camp life, and men being men, brought other problems also, not as rampant with the First Iowa as other regiments. Another of Wilkie's excerpts describes how some units policed themselves:

> In one tent of the Gov. Grays they have adopted a rule that whoever swears shall read aloud a chapter in the Bible—the book being kept constantly open for that purpose. Truth compels me to say that one can scarcely pass the tent day or night without hearing someone reading a selection of the Scriptures. Among others who are thus being benefited, I may mention my handsome young friend Charley_____, who, within the last week has read all of Genesis and Exodus and is this morning well into Leviticus, and there is a fine prospect of his finishing the entire Old Testament before the end of three months.

* * * * *

CORPORAL WILLIAM O. GULICK
FIRST IOWA CAVARLY COMPANY M

The letters and journal entries of an eighteen year old farmer/blacksmith from Clinton County who joined the First Iowa Cavalry headquartered at Camp Warren in Burlington. Gulick was wounded in action August 18, 1863, had one of his legs amputated, and on September 4th, 1863 died from the effects of the operation.

Camp Warren, Sept. 15th, 1861

....*I have seen so many strang and new things in moveing about and liveing as I have that although I am not homesick the time when I look back upon it seems long....We arrived at Burlington about 10 oclock P.M. Was marched through to dusk to Camp Warren a distance of 1 1/2 mile from town, we were met by Isaac's company and after many hearty cheers went in quarters with them for the night. This camp is very comfortable although they are nothing but shanties most of the boys sleep on the ground because they did not know how hard it would be in wet times. Friday first day in Camp Warren it rained all day so we had to stay where we could get and put up our tents. friday night it rained very hard and about midnight I found myself swimming in water with a number of others. I concluded to take quarters on a table where I took a wet but a good sleep. Saturday we put up our tents and dug ditches around them so they are water proofe....We draw as rations Pork Beef Rice Potatoes Bread sugar Coffee tea molasses vinegar Soap & candles Salt Pepper &c not all at once but all we need as evry other day for a change we have a good mess the Best one in the crowd to my notion....*

Camp Warren, Ia Sept. 29th/61
Ia Cavalry

....*My time is limited, for I am standing guard and just came off, will have to go on again at one oclock, we stand two hours on, and about four off, for twenty-four hours....We have one heavy pair Pantalonns and the promise of another soon, a very heavy Overcoat with cape a Fighting Jacket trimmed with orange a blue sack coat for a fatigue dress a pair of Boots, pair of shoes, and a hat something like Isaac's We have three Blankets one for our horse....I for-*

got to tell you all of our clothing we got Shirts two pair drawers, two pair Socks a canteen, and all the little necessaries we wanted....

Benton Barracks
Co. M 1st Ia. Cav. Oct. 19

....Tell Rich I have got a good tough horse, and well he might be for he has since I had him had the saddle on his back four days & nights with out changing Evrything has to get used to hardships When on Picket Guard a person is not allowed to unsaddle his horse....

Camp Benton, St. Louis, Mo.
Co. M. 1st Ia Cav. Oct. 27/61

....I expect we will have to be put through drilling while we stay here, we drill mostly on a trot and a gallop, and when chargeing, on a dead run. I am geting used to riding, I beleive I shall make a good horseman a number of the boys have been thrown from their horses and some been run away with I believe that not any of them have been hurt. I am proud of my horse he is such a steady good one, When I get my accouterments all on and drilling I tell you I feel animated and like fighting....We have so much cleaning to do by the way I will tell you something I have to do We have to keep our Buttons Bright (we use chalk and a brush) all our clothes brushed clean, our Boots Blacked There is a great deal of Brass about our saddles, spurs Bridles and all have to be kept Bright and clean We have Brass shoulder Plates or Appauletts our Arms &c all have to be kept Bright. We also have to keep our Quarters clean and take care of horse. We Drill five hours evry day and have dress parade at five oclock it takes about half or three fourth hours I have to cook every ten days and stand on guard once in from three to six days, we all have to get up at six oclock or Reveille, (The sound of the Bugle) and cannot go to bed until after Roll call or Tattoo (sound of the Bugle) which is at nine oclock P.M. If we do not answer at Roll Call we get a black mark, and about three markes makes extra guard duty (I never got a black mark yet)....

Benton Barracks, St. Louis, Mo.
Co. M. 1st Ia. Cav. Nov. 7/61

....The days is passed and I am again writing to you. I am quite tired to night as we have been drilling mostly on charges or on a run, and then handling a saber of 3 1/2 lbs my arm is very tired and nervous we have to drill with the saber makeing the cuts as we are on a dead run....

Benton Barracks St. Louis Mo.
Co. M. 1st Ia. Cavl. Nov.25/61

....They have sham Battles every few days in camp or out on the parade ground. I tell you it animates a person to hear thousands of muskets go off at the same time together with half doz cannon, It makes louder Thunder with ten times the Ratling you ever heard and then it is not one crash but it is kept up for some minutes first on one side and then on the other   But I am sorry to say at one of the sham fights one man had his skull on top of his head taken of by a ball that had been left in a cartridege though a mistake and all were so excited some of them shot off their ramrods one horse got piersed by a bayonett so I guess he died and one man got his leg broken by a horse kicking him so you see the excitement that prevails. Since those accidents there has not been so many sham fights....

Benton Barracks St. Louis Mo
Co M. 1st Ia, Cav. Dec 1/61

....Most of the boys were on Review today   I went out to see them it was a grand sight to see soldiers marching by Cos. two miles and a fourth long. There was about Eighteen thousand troops out today & Gen Hallock was present. I wrote Lydia about a woman being shot and guards being poisoned &c. But tonight one of the guards was shot by acsident. It was one of the Ia. 2nd boys, the guard next to him aimed his gun at him in fun, the gun proved to be loaded and the ball passed though his head. There are a great many such acsidents to happen in camp but none of the Ia. 1st have been unfortunate,

....We have cooks now for our Co. We give them both, 75 cents per month each man makeing for them about $35 apiece per month They are good Darkey cooks I tell you and it seems good to be relieved from cooking....

Benton Barracks, St. Louis Mo.
Co. M. 1st Ia. Cavl. Dec 10th/61

....*There is considerable grumbling in camp about Grub as we have done without or nearly so for two days. The last rations we drew were for Ten days and tho the time is up tomorrow we did not get our full weight as there is a fraud among some of the Quartermasters. This morning we did not Drill and this afternoon we were ordered out by our Col. Of course the boys after some hesitation went out but met the Col who only wanted to inquire about our rations. He said none of his men should go on duty with emty stomachs unless closely pressed by an enemy....*

Benton Barracks, St. Louis Mo.
Co. M 1st Ia. Cavl. Dec 12th/61

....*I can hardly compose my mind to write as the boys are talking about the Secesher they captured today. There is at the lower end of camp, or was, a saloon and sider mill some boys from the Sharpshooters on a Spree got apples and did not pay for them. The bartender to get revenge pitched on a S.S. that was standing guard and shot and stabed him so he died. This created much excitement in his Co. The saloon keeper was suspected of being a secessionist. So the Sharpshooters went to his house and after searching found a Sesesh flag. They then proseeded to tear down and burn his house mills and saloon. They were not satisfied with this but as they had received marching orders the day before they had to leave by seven oclock in the morning....*

Tuesday Jan 28th 1862

....*About Eight o'clock in the evening recd "marching orders", to be ready at Two O'clock A.M. in a short time revolvers were loaded & everything in readiness. Night set in dark & stormy, but we went early to bed to enjoy a snooze before our early departure.*

Wednesday Jan 29th 1862

Two oclock A.M. found us ready to set out on our march. The morning was stormy, the clouds hung low. It seemed to pour with more unswerving aim, the continual storm of sleet & snow on our devoted heads.

A march of four miles brought us at the Pacific R.R. depot, where we were to receive 210 prisoners. (They were soldier of the 3rd Mo. regt arrested for mutiny. They rebeled on account of change of commander) We escorted them to Benton barracks where they were lodged in guardhouse.

The march for them was tedious they wore shoes but the mud & water came over their tops. Noon found us at our quarters pretty tired, but as it was the first sweet tast of soldiering none complained.

Saturday Feb. 1st 1862

I was mounted patroll guard. I like this the best of any, as we only have to ride about the parad ground during the daytime, with orders to collect passes from pedlers. If any are minus the proper pass their goods are confiscated, generaly appropriated to the soldiers own use....

Tuesday February 11th 1862

Last night it rained consequently it is very muddy drilling, still have it to do. I was on Stable guard last night These dark nights afford great opportunity for the boys to draw chickens, geese & occasionaly a porker. A soldier of Co. K, had his nose bit off by his horse....

* * * * *

SAMUEL MAHON
SEVENTH IOWA INFANTRY COMPANY F

Taken from letters of an Ottumwa Irish twenty one year old written to his sister Elizabeth:

....The company was ordered into rendezvous at Camp Warren,

Burlington, July 12, 1861, where active training and organizing was continued. The regiment was mustered into the United States service July 24....we all had little or no money. The state furnished rations during our stay in Burlington and each man brought a blanket or comfort from home for bedding. We slept on straw in sheds and slept soundly. A jewish firm of clothiers furnished the commissioned officers of the regiment their outfit of uniform, sword, belt and other equipment, trusting them until they drew their first pay....

A week or two after we were mustered in we were ordered to St. Louis and were transported thence on a small steamboat towing two barges. The one thousand men composing the regiment filled about every available space on all three of the craft. We landed at St. Louis and were marched to Jefferson Barracks; here our arms were issued to us consisting of the old fashioned small ball muskets, caliber 72 carrying a one ounce lead spherical ball and three buck shot made up with a heavy charge of black powder. I think the officer's uniforms overtook us at St. Louis. The enlisted men, however, had no clothing except what they wore from their homes....

Samuel Mahon from Ottumwa. Captain of the 7th Iowa Infantry Company F.
(Photo Courtesy State Historical Society of Iowa—Des Moines)

* * * * *

WILLIAM S. FULTZ
11TH IOWA INFANTRY COMPANY D

Fultz worked with his father at their family sawmill located on Sugar Creek north of Moscow in Muscatine County. Fultz was 25 when he enlisted in the Eleventh Iowa Infantry as fouth corporal on September 19, 1861. He recorded the daily events of his service in a diary and later used his diary to compose the following excerpt from his memoirs:

> *We reached Davenport after dark [Oct. 1 or 2, 1861] and each man receaved a blanket from the state issued by Adjutant General Baker after which we were escorted to Camp by Rev. Whetlesey who afterward became our regimental chaplain....*
> *On the 3d day of October we were mustered into U.S. Service four of our boys being rejected on account of disabilaty....*
> *On the 26th of October we receaved our first uniforms and on the 27th our knapsacks and haversacks and canteens and on the 29th our guns and accoutrements. The guns were the old fashioned Harpers ferry musket pattern flint locks changed to percussion locks. That same day the people from along Sugar Creek came up to camp with wagon loads of good things and gave us a regular basket picnic in our quarters it being wet and rainy out of doors....*
> *On the first day of November we receaved our state pay counting from the time that we enlisted until October 3rd when we were mustered into U.S. service....*

* * * * *

PETER WILSON
14TH IOWA INFANTRY COMPANY G

Excerpts from the letters of a twenty four year old farmer of Scottish descent living in the Wolf Creek settlement of northern Tama county:

> *Camp McClellan*
> *Oct 25th, 1861*
>
> *We were welcomed with the rousing cheers of some 3000 men. We were marched into our quarters and I was rather struck with*

the appearance of them. Our shanties are made as tight as a good barn, bunked up like a ship two in a bunk. We have plenty of straw and we are very comfortable. Our fare consists of beef, bread, beans, potatoes, rice and coffee, we get plenty to eat and good enough. We are all satisfied with our camp arrangements.... We drill 3 hours per day and it is different from our old drill in the guards. I could hardly believe how much we learn....We are up in the morning at daylight and march down to the river to wash. The sentinels are posted around the camp at short intervals muskets in hand and no soldier can get out without a pass or with a commissioned officer. If any one gets on the spree or misbehaves in any way he is put into the guard house; one got in tonight for stealing a pipe and another for stealing a pie. There is a great variety of character among 3000 men. At present some are writing, some are fiddling, dancing, fifing, drumming, playing cards, singing hymns, songs &c, some are reading the Bible, some the newspapers some studying tactics, every one to his fancy, everything goes on agreeable. I have not seen a quarrel since we came into camp....

Camp Benton
Dec 2nd, 1861

....We have just come in from a three hours drill in the snow. There was just enough snow to make us slip and slide and tumble. There were so many companies drilling all around us that we could scarcely mind our own business. There is an incredible amount of maneuvers going on in drill hours. The drill ground is some two miles square and in Company Drill there seems to be scarcely room for the exercises. There is Flying Artillery which as near as I can describe looks something like Klingiman's big wagon with six splendid horses hitched to it, the nigh horses mounted, the gunners sitting on the box on the front axle where the ammunition is kept. The cannon is mounted on the hind axle. They gallop from one place to another, firing blank cartridges at the Cavalry to get the horses used to the noise. There are some splendid Cavalry Regiment in camp, their horses are generally light, fiery, prancing nags. They are well fed and ridden very hard. They mostly stand in the open air but they have good blankets. There seems to be plenty of food and clothing for man and beast....A good many of the Regs. have got so far along with their drill as to use the bugle in giving

commands. That is what they use on the battle field. It is a splendid sight to see a well-drilled regiment drilling with their commander so far away that his voice could not he heard. I saw a company of Sharpshooters going through their exercises this morning. They were a good looking lot of men and seemed to understand their drill which is entirely different from ours. I would not say anything against Cap. Stivers in the Company as that is against the rules but if ever we come to the field of battle we will send him to stay with the women where he spends most of his time now. He has not drilled us once since we enlisted, in fact he don't seem to care how we get along. Our Lieutenants are very different, they take pride in having us the best drilled Company in the Regt. which we are said to be....

Camp Benton
Dec 3d, 1861

....The barracks are built in rows about a mile on each side with sundry others across the ends. Each barrack contains two Companies. They are about 40 feed wide and seventy feet long, one large stove in the centre which keeps the place quite comfortable. The front door opens on the parade ground which is perfectly level and about a mile square, the back door opens on the row of kitchen buildings. The dining room is roofed but not sided up, the cook houses are the next row. Each Company does their own cooking, some hire darkies to cook for them. We pay three of our own boys to cook for us, we pay them 12 dollars per month each....Behind the cook houses are the Cavalry horses....The Cavalry boys have more work than we do, it takes them all their time to keep their things in order while we generally with the exception of drill hours spoiling for something to do. We fill up the time pleasantly enough....

Dec 7th, 1861....I think our Colonel, Major, Adjutant, and Lieutenant Colonel are all men that understand their business and as far as I have seen are men in the highest sense of the word. They come among the boys occasionally, use us like equals. When in the ranks they of course show their dignity. I have never seen an officer insult a private since I enlisted. Some of them probably would if they dared to do so but it is all day with them if they lose the good will of the men. As a proof of this our boys got to thinking Stivers was paying more attention to his women than he ought and *neglecting to drill us as much as he ought. They got up a petition requesting him to resign or tend to his business; he took the latter course double quick time. If he is not very careful our First Lieutenant will be in his place before long....There is some fun breaking mules and horses but they do it up in business style and I believe there are some of the best teamsters here that I have seen.*

Benton Barracks Jan 23, 1862

....We have a good many shines to relieve the monotony of camp life. There is an old big Dutchman that has been furnishing some of the lovers of something good to drink with lager beer. The other day as he was passing along behind our quarters our Major slugged him, got into the wagon which contained some fifteen or twenty kegs of beer. He took out the end board and pulled the kegs out on the ground. The old major was jumping mad and went into the cook house to get an axe to kick the ends out of the kegs. By this time a great crowd had collected and the kegs by some unaccountable means began rapidly to disappear. By the time the Major got ready to smash the kegs there was none to be found. He immediately began to search for the lost kegs. Some of them he found, mostly empty by this time. He was determined to make an example of some one and continued his search. He came into our quarters and found a keg to all appearances. He pulled out the plug and strange to tell instead of beer pure water gurgled out. The Major left, amongst ill oppressed laughter. The beer had been drunk and the men, liking some fun, filled the keg with water hiding it where he would be sure to find it. We have some good jokes but they won't hardly pay for writing....

* * * * *

BENJAMIN F. THOMAS
14TH IOWA INFANTRY COMPANY G

The recollections of another young lad from Wolf Creek who enlisted along with Peter Wilson. He begins with their arrival in Camp McClellan in October, 1861:

....Finally we arrived at Davenport. Cheering, cheering cheering on every side. Two other companies who came from the western part of the State were on the train with us. We were all dismounted from the cars and formed into line, and, headed by a brass band, marched out to Camp McClellan. This was a new camp about two miles from Davenport on the Mississippi....

On the morning of October 24th the boom of the morning gun aroused us and we rushed out of the barracks to see what was the matter. We found the older companies all in line and the Orderly Sergeants caling the roll....

The rules of the camp were for us to arise at six o'clock A. M., answer to role-call, then march down to the river and wash our hands and faces in the mighty Mississippi. Just think of it, the Father of Waters for a wash bowl! Return to camp. Breakfast call. After breakfast, sick call and guard mount and then company drill for two hours. By this time we were ready for dinner. After dinner was company drill again, and at sunset dress parade....

October 29th....The company in the barracks next to us was mustered into the United States service and two of their men refused to take the oath of allegiance. They were ordered to be drummed out of the camp. Thirty of their comrads formed a hollow square with the two men within. A martial band followed playing the "Rogues March". They marched through the principal streets of our camp and to the main entrance. Then the officer in charge gave each of the "Rogues" a lusty kick and bade them "be gone". Poor fellows! The band then returned to their quarters playing "Yankee Doodle" with all the vim their instruments were capable of.

Monday, November 18th....A company of the Thirteenth Iowa Regiment that came from Benton County was in the barrack just across the street from us. To this company belonged Buren R. Sherman and Ward Sherman, his brother, and some other boys we know well. They had a space in their barrack large enough to dance in and frequently had us there to dance with them. A boy with a handkerchief tied around his arm represented a girl. One of our boys from Toledo, Josiah Luke, was about the best violinist I ever heard. He frequently made the music for us. Card playing was the principal pastime for the boys, but I did not play.

Buren R. Sherman from Vinton. A member of the 13th Iowa Infantry Company G, Governor of Iowa 1882-1886
(Photo Courtesy State Historical Society of Iowa—Des Moines)

Ward B. Sherman from Buckingham. A member of the 13th Iowa Infantry Company G, later 1st Lieutenant and Commissary of the 9th Iowa Cavalry.
(Photo Courtesy State Historical Society of Iowa—Des Moines)

November 20th. Our first episode of real military life occurred last night. The Thirteenth Regiment was ordered to march today. Many of their men took the opportunity to run the guards and spend the night in a carousal in Davenport. Captain Stivers was officer of the day, which fact gave him command of the camp. When he learned of the boys escaping to the city he thought he would have some fun. He came to our barrack about eleven o'clock and called ten of us to go with him and arrest everyone we could find. The Captain took us to a place where he expected to find some of the boys. In a large room several girls finely attired were playing cards or chatting with a number of soldiers or citizens. We compelled the soldiers to show their passes which everyone did. From there we went to many other places of like character. At one house as we entered we saw some soldiers run up the stairs. Eleazar Stoakes and I followed them and when we got to the top of the stairs they ran into two of the bed rooms. I followed one and caught him. Stoakes lost his man but when he thrust his gun under a bed the man called out that he would surrender. About this time my prisoner got mad and swore at us in a terrible manner. But he had to go just the same. These, with some the other boys caught, were marched back to camp and placed in the guard house....One Lieutenant of Company K, William K. Kirkwood was a nephew of the Governor. We were called "Kirkwood pets"....

Shadrock Haskins M.D., from Cass Center. Asst. Surgeon of the 14th Iowa Infantry.
(Photo Courtesy of State Historical Society of Iowa–Des Moines)

* * * * *

CYRUS F. BOYD
15TH IOWA INFANTRY REGIMENT COMPANY G

C. F. Boyd, a twenty four year old from Indianola, wrote a profuse diary of his soldiering and camp life exploits. His camp life excerpts begin with his experiences in Camp Halleck at Keokuk:

Oct 24th Our fears are quieted as regards clothes. We have been required to throw away, give away or otherwise dispose of our citizens dress and we to-day drew from a Quarter-Master down on Johnston street a complete suit of Army blue The clothes we think are very nice and we are as proud as peacocks of our appearance How we pity those poor miserable fellows at home No new clothes because they will not go soldiering Here we are having lots of fun and glory....

Dec. 12th The interval between dates herein has been occupied in company drill and the duties of Camp life which are monotonous enough Taken off the farms as the most of us have been and shut up in a pen as we are is enough to kill the best of us Measles and other diseases have reduced our numbers for drill almost one half and many of the men are sick....

Feby 22d....Mud deep and growing deeper Uniforms in bad plight—feet wet and cold and patriotism down to zero. After dusk I took a walk up town in the immediate neighborhood of the Catholic Church and stayed until 12 o'clock M As I came back met a drunk soldier on the high side walk near the Church He made a mis-slip and rolled off and down the clay bank clear to the bottom gutter I did not stop to enquire if he got his clothes soiled or not. I think the next morning will show that they were not only soiled but subsoiled I heard a grave voice at the bottom swearing that it would be "a brick house and forty dollars in money" whatever that may mean Arrived safely at Camp and with the pass word passed the guard and fell into my bunk

Feby 25th....Last night the men had high old times running from the Patrol guard Some of them were caught and are now in the "guard house" for several hours or days as the case may be Some of them are getting pretty old at the business of running the quard The Patrol has to do some good running to overtake these night fellows The patrol sometimes find men away from Camp two miles in saloons and disreputable houses There are some bad men in Co's "A

61

& H"....
March 17th   Everybody is excited   We received orders to prepare to leave Keokuk   To draw three days rations and to be ready at a moments notice to embark. Destination unknown   Extra Cooks were detailed and things are being hurried on....

March 18th   Weather cloudy and wet. If certain boats come up tonight we shall leave to-morrow   Have been very busy all day This afternoon we marched with Knapsacks on   We find that we shall have a mules load to carry—2 blankets, extra clothing and a big overcoat, haversack &c saying nothing about a gun and ammunition

Tie Shepard and I took tea with Miss Lizzie Sullivan Miss Hart was there and we had a good time   Never were men treated so well as we have been by the good people of Keokuk They have all seemed to study the interests and the happiness of the soldiers and have provided every comfort that can be imagined   They have used us too well and we will suffer for it when we leave here Came past the Miss Grahams and bid them good-bye   The Johnston girls gave us some ginger snaps and I have my haversack full of provisions

Miss River—on board the "Jennie Deans"

March 19th....The rain was falling in torrents as we marched down Main street   But notwithstanding this all the side walks were crowded with people   All the windows were full of children waiving flags and handkerchiefs....1000 strong we marched that afternoon in the pride and glory of youthful soldiers The sound of the music- the cheering shouts of the people robbed us of all regrets and we marched proudly away. I saw some of our good friends on the side walks—but it would not do to look back We were marched on board the "Jennie Deans" and crowded like cattle into every conceivable corner

"Benton Barracks" St Louis

March 24th   This has been a fine day and we have improved by drilling   A number of the 7th Wis got drunk and the officers had a great time to manage them....

Men selling "bullet proof" vests were in camp to-day The boys say our Capt purchased one   They submitted some for trial about *one half of them were bored through with musket balls They sold for $8.00 to $16.00 If the bullet did not go through it would knock a man into the middle of next week so that he might as well be killed first as last*

* * * * *

CLINTON PARKHURST
16TH IOWA INFANTRY COMPANY C

Recollections of an 18 year old from LeClaire who enlisted on February 12, 1862. Parkhurst provides a good depiction of the soldierly experience at Benton Barracks, or Camp Benton as it was called:

In the spring of 1862, Camp Benton, just west of St. Louis, was a rallying point for the volunteers of the Northwest. Fifteen or twenty thousand new troops occupied it, in tents and barracks; brass bands paraded; raw cavalrymen, with unstained sabres, stood in long lines learning to cut, thrust and "let the enemy parry"; infantry with glittering weapons were drilling in companys and in regiments; the silver ringing of bright ramrods in still brighter gun-barrels was heard on every hand; staff officers, who had been clerks or unfledged lawyers a few weeks previously, galloped about with an air of immense responsibility, as though a battle were in progress. All was glitter, bustle, and excitement. "Now, this is war", I said to myself, leaning against a cannon that had never been fired, and folding my arms in the fashion of Napoleon.

In a couple of days a great number of boxes somewhat resembling coffins, were hauled to the front of our quarters, and we turned out with loud cheers to "draw guns". They were beautiful Springfield rifles, as bright as silver, and of the best pattern used in either army during the war. It was an exciting moment. When the orderly sergeant handed me one, together with a belt, a bayonet and sheath, a cap-box, the cartridge box, and a brass "U.S." to put on the cartridge box, I felt that a great trust was being reposed in me by the United States governement. Many a man has gone to Congress or received a Major-General's commission with less actual modesty and solemn emotion than I experienced on that occasion. And that burnished rifle, so beautiful that it seemed fit only to stand in the corner of a parlor, or repose in a case of rosewood and velvet, subsequently had an obscure but worthy history. In the course of the war, from its well-grooved barrel, I hurled more than eight hundred Minie balls in protest against a Southern Confederacy, and on my last battlefield I smashed it against the side of an oak tree, that it might never fire a shot for the dissolution of the Union.

Still other things were rapidly given to us. We received those horrible-looking regulation felt hats which somebody decreed we must wear; also black plumes to adorn them; a brass eagle that resembled a peacock in full feather, for the side of a hat; a brass bugle for the front; brass letters and figures to denote each man's company and regiment; leather "dog collars" to span our necks, and much other trumpery-all of which we threw away eventually, except the hat. The latter, in time, we lowered a story or two, by an ingenious method, and it served us well in storms of rain, and in the fierce heats of Southern summer. Buttoned and belted and strapped, and profusely ornamented, we felt we were soldiers indeed, and we pined for gory combat. Now and then a straggler would arrive, and after gazing on our splended parapheranalia, he would be in a fever of anxiety until he, too, had secured the last gewgaw to which he was entitled at the hands of a generous Government. "Have you drawed your bugle yet?" became the slang salutation of the camp, the original inquiry having been propounded by an alarmed rural volunteer to one of his belated companions. After strutting about with our new weapons, like so many boys in their first new boots, we were ordered to the drill-ground to learn how to handle them without impaling one another.

Early the next morning the drums rattled furiously, and orders came to pack up instanter and get ready to leave for the seat of war. The wildest commotion ensued. Every other matter was forgotten, and with eager haste we got into line on the parade ground. There we learned the most annoying duty of a soldier -to stand in his place like a hitching post, perhaps for hours, simply awaiting orders.

We finally stacked arms and had breakfast, but at eleven o'clock we marched out of Camp Benton with drums beating and colors flying, going we knew not where. Three batteries and three regiments of infantry followed us. The people of St. Louis cheered us vociferously all along the route. At 2 o'clock we reached the steamboat levee, and our regiment (16th Iowa) was packed and crowded on board a miserable old craft called the Crescent City. The other regiments embarked on other boats, and more troops and batteries were swiftly ferried across from East St. Louis and embarked on still other steamers. At dusk our somewhat imposing flotilla swung off, and amid the roar and clatter of martial music, and the cheering of soldiers and people, we steamed down the Mississippi. It was the 1st of April, and our commanders told us we would smell gunpowder soon.

* * * * *

CHARLES ALLEY
5TH IOWA CAVALRY COMPANY C

Alley was from Brownsville, just across the border in the territory of Nebraska. He enlisted in the military in Iowa and was sent to Benton Barracks where he became a member of a unit known as "The Curtis Horse" which was designated Company C of the Fifth Iowa Cavalry.

(Oct) 15th....Last night some of the men stole some chickens & had quite a feast. How wicked! Going to hazard their lives in war & steal. God grant that they may feel their wickedness and repent.

Oct. 21, 1861....And now I must say a few words on the pleasures & pains of camp life. It is very pleasant in fine weather & quite the reverse in wet. In the morning before day we generally have breakfast. It is quite a sight to see the dark forms of the men moving among the white tents & the bright fires. The cooks stooping over their pans & pots, now rubbing their eyes smarting from smoke; now drawing back suddenly as the wind drives a burst of flames in their faces; all this with the others moving round in anxious waiting for the call to breakfast with their forms now bright as the fires flame up, now dark as it dies away; makes quite an animated scene. Well breakfast comes at last, & then there is a general scramble as there are not enough cups, plates, &c, and nobody hardly wants to be last. Presently all are eating with the keen relish caused by such an open air life. Those who are to do on guard, hurriedly for fear of the Bugle calling them to their posts before finishing. But hark! The bugle! Plates cups &c. are thrown aside, a grumble or two, a muttered imprecation or more likely a volley of them & the guards fall in and are marched to their posts. But there is one comfort, as comrads will take each one's place and let him finish after a while so the disappointment is only temporary....

30 Oct. Today we reach St. Louis about 8 o'clock and we were marched directly to Benton Barracks, where we now are. The part of the camp where we are quartered is laid off in the form of a square; a long line of sheds on each side of it for soldiers, back of these the kitchens & sheds for the soldiers to eat in. Altogether it looks as if it would do very well for men who are soon to take to the field to live in. Thus ends our first stage....

Sunday, Nov. 10th, 1861. I have been here for some time and I must confess I find things worse than I expected. Oh! what wickedness, evil in every shape, moral degredation everywhere showing itself....So many men gathered together to fight in their country's cause and almost no effort to lead them to Christ....

Nov 13, 61. Things have been quite busy in camp thus far this week. Training of horses to run up on the muskets and to the mouths of the cannons, while firing and also being drawn up in line when the foot would charge on them with muskets & fixed bayonets. They have been some time used to hearing the artillery at a distance. Also, but not so much, the musketry. It is surprising how well they stand all the noise &c. From these movements I would infer that they must be preparing these troops for the field. Troops are coming in and going out constantly.... We had an election last evening for sergeant. I do not very well like the one elected. He being a man who by his own account would never come into the army if he could have got better wages out of it, & would leave it any time for higher wages if he could. A poor patriot surely for this fellow soldier to delight to honor! And here I say en passant, that I would have been proposed but I was an Irishman & was too religious....

Nov. 17. On Friday two horsees threw their riders & each of these had a leg broken. One of the men of the seventh Iowa had the top of his head blown off, killing him instantly; such are sad accompaniments of war....

* * * * *

JACOB CARROLL SWITZER
22ND IOWA INFANTRY COMPANY A.

The memoirs of an eighteen year old farm boy from Johnson County:

I ought to give a sketch of camp life at "Camp Pope," Iowa City, where my soldier life began. Camp Pope was located on the east side of Summit Street from North of Bowery Street to the Rock Island railroad. The parade and drill ground was on both sides of the railroad up to the front of Governor Kirkwood's house on Kirkwood Avenue. We were all heroes in the eyes of our mothers, sisters, and cousins. With wooden bayonets we challenged the salute of the wooden sword of the officer of the guard as that dignitary made his grand rounds night or day. We halted the fierce school boy as he endeavored to "run the guard line" with his basket of homemade candy, fruit or pies to sell to the unwary veteran for his delectation. We made the day vibrate with the calls of "Corporal of the Guard, Post Number Nine"....

It was with a very squemish stomach that I first took my tin cup, tin plate, tin spoon, and iron knife and fork and went to the soup house for my rations. I looked at the cooks, greasy, dirty. slovenly; and then at the provisions and wondered of what the soup was composed. It didn't seem to me just like "Mother used to cook" but whether I ate it or not the meal time only lasted a few minutes and I had other things to think of. One day Mother and the girls and neighbor's girls set us a dinner of good things outside the lines-such as we saw so little of for many weary months after.

* * * * *

CAPTAIN C. A. LUCAS
24TH IOWA INFANTRY COMPANY D

Charles Alexander Lucas was from Iowa City and had served in the Belgium Military previous to the Civil War. He wrote nearly one hundred letters to his brother Henry Joseph Lewis during the war. In one of his letters, Captain Lucas provides some interesting insight into the admission and training standards of the Civil War, and a little camp rivalry that he was involved in:

St. Louis, Mo., October 22, 1862.

My Dear Brother Henry:—I thought I would write you of a few of the most important incidents that have transpired since I left home.

On September 4, Messrs. John Parrot and Jesse Westenhaver came to our camp, and next morning they paid the Johnson County boys the fifty dollars county bounty due them. I sent you forty dollars through the kindness of Mr. John Parrott, who will hand it to you at the first opportunity. We are having drill twice a day, and the boys are improving fast, rather faster than I expected. They are anxious to learn, and I begin to feel proud of them....

On September 18 we were mustered into the United States service. I often think how the regimental surgeon and the U.S. mustering officer, Captain H. B. Hendershott, examined us. We did not have to strip off all garments as they did in the Belgian army; we did not even have to take off our coats. All we had to do was to march, one by one, before the mustering officer, with our hands raised above our heads, and work our fingers.

On September 30, I had an interview with Captain Wilson of the regular army, who had been appointed to drill the 24th Iowa, in battalion drill; and as I could see that the regiment was not improving very fast, I suggested to him to assemble officers at the Colonel's headquarters, once a day, and to have a black-board there, and explain to them, the different movements of the school of the battalion. He did so, but he had served mostly in cavalry, and not very long in infantry, and as he could see that I understood the movements full as well as he did, he asked me to help him in that. I did so, and the regiment improved faster after that....

During the last two weeks that we were in Camp Strong, I had the name of being one of the best drilled man, especially in sword and bayonet exercise, in the two regiments—the 24th and the 35th Iowa—that were there; and right here I must tell you of an incident that was rather amusing, not only to myself, but to the boys of the 24th Iowa, who were there at the time. As I was sergeant of the guard at the gate, on the 7th instant, my Captain came to me and said that I was invited to the Colonel's headquarters of the 35th Iowa, by Captain Flanagan of that regiment, who had served for several years in the United States army. I reported there immediately, and saw at least one thousand men from both regiments, who had come to witness the fencing match. I was introduced to Captain Flannigan, who had two wooden swords in his hands. He handed one of them to me, but as it was not customary for a commissioned and non-commisioned officer to have that kind of sport with their uniforms on, I took off my dess-coat, and he did the same. We then saluted each other with the sword, and got "on guard." I then told him: "Go Ahead." He tried a few thrusts and cuts or strokes, but I parried every one. Then I went for him, and struck him nearly every time. We were at it about ten minutes, when the boys of the 24th were cheering pretty well, while those of the 35the were rather quiet. I could see that the Captain looked somewhat disappointed at not doing away with me so easily as he expected. I sympathized with him, but at the same time I did not want to let him have the best of me. He soon saluted with the sword again, and said "that will do," and the cheers that went up from the 24th made me feel good. The Captain shook hands with me again, and even complimented me, but he never invited me after that. I suppose he thought he was the best swordsman around, but I think he found out there is a little sergeant in the 24th Iowa, who is a match for him.

Camp Strong was nice and level; very nice for drilling, dress parade, guard mounting, etc., but there was too much swampy land near it, which made it unhealthy, and besides that I think there were too many loads of melons brought into camp....

October 20, we left Camp Strong, and got on board the steamer "Hawk-Eye State." Our destination was St. Louis. October 22 about 8:30 A. M. we arrived in St. Louis. The same day, about noon, we left the "Hawk-Eye State," and went on board the "Empress," where I am now writing to you.

Town square of Newton at the time of Civil War enlistment.
(Photo Courtesy State Historical Society of Iowa—Des Moines)

MAINTAINING THE SUPPLY OF SOLDIERS

It soon became obvious the war that some speculated would last only three months was going to last longer and require more than just a token enlistment of volunteer troops for a short period of time. On May 3, 1861, President Lincoln issued a proclamation calling for an additional military force. On May 16th the War Department ordered the organization of two more regiments in Iowa. Governor Kirkwood immediately sent the Second Infantry Regiment to rendezvous at Keokuk on May 25th, and ordered the Third Infantry Regiment to be there by June 3rd.

Following the President's second call for troops and mustering of the Second and Third Infantry Regiments, Iowa was tapped for additional troops. The Fourth Iowa Infantry was mustered in on August 8, 1861; the Fifth on July 15th, 16th and 17th; the Sixth on July 17th and 18th, the Seventh Iowa Infantry completed muster on August 2, 1861 and the Second Iowa Cavalry was mustered into United States service at Davenport on August 25, 1861. A few prominent individuals had the moxy to form their own regiments. The Eighth Iowa Infantry, known as H.B. Hoffman's regiment, was mustered in at Davenport under Colonel Frederick Steele about the first of September. Another known as Vandever's regiment formed the Ninth Iowa Infantry and completed muster at Dubuque on September 24, 1861. The Tenth Iowa Infantry, raised by J.C. Bennett, was mustered in at Iowa City under Colonel

Nicholas Pereczel with Bennett as major on September 6th and 7th. Six companies of the First Iowa Cavalry were in camp near Burlington in July, the remainder came during the following month with the regiment reaching full organization the last of August and mustering in the first part of September.

Lt. James H. Miller (left) and Sgt. William P. Latimer, both from Indianola, and of the 10th Iowa Infantry Company G.

Cavalry regiments were easier to raise than infantry. It was highly desirable to ride a horse in the long travels of military units rather than endure the agonizing marches of the infantry. However, cavalry soldiers had the additional duties of caring for horses. The people of Iowa were particularly anxious for cavalry regiments to be mustered in order that they would have an opportunity to sell the necessary horses, the only product they had that was in demand by the government.

On October 2nd Governor Kirkwood wrote Secretary Cameron that he was organizing the Eleventh and Twelfth Iowa Infantry Regiments and the Fourth Cavalry Regiment. Recruiting was also in process for the Thirteenth and Fourteenth Infantry. The Secretary of War replied that he was willing to receive all the troops Iowa could furnish for active duty.

Band of the 11th Iowa Infantry.
(Photo Courtesy State Historical Society of Iowa—Iowa City)

As the war ground on into 1862, demand for troops never ceased. Muster of the Fifteenth Infantry Regiment was completed on February 22, 1862, and the Sixteenth Infantry Regiment on March 12, 1862. The Seventeenth completed muster on April 16, 1862 and left the state on the 19th of April for St. Louis. These regiments were not resplendent with the states young men who comprised earlier regiments, they were made up of older men, many of whom were married, and had children. It was a sign that volunteering was beginning to suffer, and indeed it was. The war was more serious than had been anticipated, and much of the gallant enthusiasm present in the early days of the war had subsided. Furthermore, disloyal sentiment had grown rampant in some parts of the State. In Henry County a recruiting officer was attacked and threatened with being hanged. A secret organization known as the Knights of the Golden Circle was formed, partly for the purpose of discouraging enlistments. The organization was composed of southern sympathizers, reapers of war profits, and slackers.

Forming new regiments now required more effort and a change in tactics to maintain the flow of enlistees. Recruiting parties composed of two commissioned officers and four non-commissioned officers or privates from each regiment toured the country enlisting volunteers. A premium of two dollars was paid to the recruiters for each recruit accepted.

Incentives, or inducements as they were called, became the vogue for attracting volunteers as the war continued its ceaseless sapping of the state's willing men. Of all the inducements, bounties were probably the most effective.

General orders issued later in war provided a bounty of $100 for every volunteer when he was discharged. Wounded volunteers were entitled to the same benefits as were accorded soldiers in the regular army. If a soldier was killed or died, his heirs would receive the $100. Bounties no doubt provided some incentive, when the wage of privates at $11 to $16 a month is considered. But the anticipation of pocketing $100 when they were discharged was so indefinitely remote, that with most volunteers this bounty probably had slight effect on recruiting.

Bounties did not, however, end with the Union's commitment. States, counties, cities, organizations, even wealthy individuals offered up additional bounties as further incentives. No bounties were offered by the State of Iowa during the entire war, but incidents of bounties in counties, cities, or by private subscription did occur. To make bounties and incentives more enticing, Congress in 1862 made the first month's salary of a recruit payable in advance, and on July 7th of the same year, upon the urgent request of William H. Seward, (Secretary of State), the War Department issued orders to pay $25 of the $100 bounty at the time of muster. Still another means of stimulating enlistments was devised in 1862. A premium of two dollars was paid to any person for every recruit obtained. Or, if the volunteer presented himself in person the premium was payable to him.

As a result of these incentives, many men rushed to the Union call, but only wherever they could obtain the largest bounties. Large cities and wealthy counties drained the surrounding country and received credit for volunteers who had residence elsewhere, thus avoiding the threatened draft quotas. As a consequence, when the draft was ordered, the rural districts and backward counties had to furnish men in place of those for whom credit should have been received to begin with.

As early as 1862, signs of the evils created by the bounty system began to show. Soldiers whose financial motivation overruled patriotism were a definite lower caliber soldier. General W. T. Sherman observed that men who were prompted to volunteer at the beginning of the war by the spirit of loyalty and patriotism were the best soldiers—better than the bounty-paid gamblers, better than the conscripts, and far better than the paid substitutes that filled the ranks in the later years. General Grant also became exasperated with the dilatory tactics of the recruiting officials. In

September (1864) he wrote of the bounty motivated recruits, "The men we have been getting in this way nearly all desert, and out of five reported North as having enlisted we don't get more than one effective soldier." In a letter written home on June 23, 1863 from Fort Halleck in Columbus, KY., Clerk L. W. Shilton of Co. I, 14th Iowa Infantry wrote:

> ....*The old soldiers of the 14th were very anxious to know how hard the Draft blows in Iowa, and if there is any prospect of those who yet remain behind of being blown over the line, I mean "Drafted in the army"! and also, they hardley know whether that new company is Drafted Militia, Conscripts, or Volunteers....*
>
> *The 31st Wisconsin Drafted Militia is here, they are true conscripts, they are afforded to stand picket guard only 3 or 4 miles from here where there is no wisky to distract them, they can drill very well, and make a very fine appearance on dress parade, but the name Secesh scares them, many of them will run from a black stump at night. They will do to stand guard in camp under the eyes of their officers but for any field service they are of little service....*

None of the financial incentives had the affect of the government's threatened draft in August of 1862. Following the threat Governor Kirkwood reported; "Our whole State appears to be volunteering...."Some counties averaged a company a week. Only women, old men, and boys remained at home in some Iowa communities, the rest had gone of to war.

In response to the Government's call for troops on July 2 and August 4, 1862, Iowa furnished twenty-two regiments of infantry-the Nineteenth to Fortieth Regiments inclusive, over 20,000 troups in just one month's time! As in 1861, regiments were formed with the idea of appealing to particular classes. Colonel E. C. Byam raised a "temperance regiment" which became the Twenty-fourth Iowa Infantry. Perhaps the most famous of all was the "Governor's Grey-Beards." This regiment of "active and vigorous" men, the 37th Iowa Infantry, consisted of enlisties older than the enlistment age limit of 45. It was the only regiment of its kind in the entire Union Army! Eighty year old Curtis King of Muscatine volunteered, and was accepted, and was the oldest man to serve in the Union Army. The regiment brought not only fathers, but even the grandfathers of Iowa sons, into the war effort. A total of 1300 sons and grandsons of the Greybeards served in the Union Army.

Private Peter W. Coleman (left) and Wagoner Michael W. Coleman, both from Cedar Rapids, and of the 31st Iowa Infantry Company A.
(Photos Courtesy State Historical Society of Iowa—Iowa City)

Lt. Col. Ed Wright (left) from Springdale and Major Leander Clark from Buckingham of the 24th Iowa Infantry.
(Photos Courtesy State Historical Society of Iowa—Des Moines)

Dog that went through the war with the 23rd Iowa Infantry.
(Photo Courtesy State Historical Society of Iowa—Des Moines)

The greatest financial boon to volunteers came on June 25, 1863 when the Veteran Volunteer Army was created. To all volunteers who had served at least nine months, and who would reenlist for three years, there was offered one month's advance pay, a two dollar premium, and a bounty of $400 payable in $25, $50, and $75 installments. In October the bounty for a raw recruit to fill vacancies in old regiments was raised to $300, and at the same time the premium offered for volunteers was increased to $15 for one without military experience and $25 for a veteran. Some veterans who had served earlier in the war and had retired back to civilian life took advantage of the incentive and reenlisted.

Officers of the 36th Iowa Infantry.
(Photo Courtesy State Historical Society of Iowa—Des Moines)

Problems also confronted the State of Iowa that demanded protective measures for its own citizens. Indians to the North and West, and marauding troops of secesionists in Northern Missouri threatened Iowa citizens. Governor Kirkwood sent out a circular letter in October, 1861, suggesting that companies and regiments of militia be raised for the "better protection of the exposed borders of this State, to resist marauding parties of Indians and other hostile person, to repel invasion, and to render prompt and efficient assistance to the United States." On September 9, 1862, an act approved by the Ninth General Assembly authorized organization of a force of not less than five hundred mounted men from the counties most convenient for the protection of the northwest. Five companies were organized. Together with the previously organized Sioux City Cavalry Company, these troops were known as the Northern Border Brigade and numbered about 250 men. A Southern Border Brigade was organized in the autumn of 1862. This force of State troops was organized into four battalions with two companies in the first and second battalions and three in the third and fourth. Every day ten men were detailed from each company to police Iowa's southern border. Every man furnishished his own clothing, horse, equipment, and arms.

Recruiting in Iowa during the summer and fall of 1863 resulted in the formation of the Eighth and Ninth cavalry, the Fourth Light Artillery, and the First African Infantry. The Sixth and Seventh Cavalry had completed their organization on March 5, 1863, and July 25, 1863, respectively. The Eighth Cavalry was mustered into Federal service on September 1st. At the urgent request of Governor Kirkwood the organization of the Ninth Cavalry was approved on September 7th and the muster was completed on November 30, 1863. The place of rendezvous for both regiments was Camp Roberts near Davenport. The Fourth Artillery, numbering one hundred and fifty two men rank and file, was mustered into the United States service at Davenport on November 23, 1863.

First Lt. Daniel D. Smock, 1st Iowa Vol. Infantry of African Desent. Smock was from Benton County and had originally served in the 13th Infantry Company G
(Photo Courtesy State Historical Society of Iowa—Iowa City, from Rev. Starr Collection)

In 1864, to relieve seasoned troops from mundane duties so they could fulfill urgent needs for troops in the war fronts, the government authorized raising regiments for which the term of enlistment was only 100 days. Iowa raised four regiments and one battalion of 100 day soldiers, the Forty-fourth, Forty-fifth, Forty-sixth, and Forty-seventh Regiments and the Forty-eighth Battalion. These regiments were assigned to various guard and garrison duties and were the last regiments raised in Iowa for the Civil War.

Francis M. Peabody from Newton, 17 year old Drummer Boy of the 22nd Iowa Infantry Company C. (left) David C. Martin from Linn County, 16 year old Drummer Boy of the 31st Iowa Infantry Company A.
(Photos Courtesy State Historical Society of Iowa—Iowa City)

A RECRUITMENT STORY

Apparently the various enticements offered to officers for recruiting new soldiers became competitive on occassion. This story from the Fayette County Newspaper, PIONEER in West Union is testimony.

ARMY CORRESPONDENCE

BENTON BARRACKS, ST. LOUIS Mo.
Dec. 22, 1861

MR. HURD—My Dear Sir:...You have doubtless before heard this about "Jack in the box." I see a version of it in the PIONEER which is false; and lest my friends in Eldorado should get a wrong impression of the affair, I give you a history of it. At West Union I enlisted a Dutch stage driver whose name is Nick Dubbnell. Some days afterwards while at Elkader he came across a Sergeant and a Corporal of the 16th Regular Infantry, who were also recruiting. After having made themselves quite friendly with Nick, caroused all night with him, and got him to imbibe quite freely, they succeeded in convincing him, to use his own English , that "ter regulars kits besser crub, besser cloden, an besser every ting ish te volunteers." Under this impression he signed their roll and took the oath. Their next care was to provide him with clothing, which is a custom in the regular army. But their supply was exhausted on other recruits; and those enterprising non commissioned officers accordingly took the outer raiment from their own backs, and gave them to the Dutchman in exchange for his—the Sergeant I believe sparing his cap and coat, and the Corporal, his pants. Nick then returned to West Union; and when I had informed him that he was my man and that I should have him, he became suddenly intoxicated with the idea of going with me to St. Louis and getting another suit of uniform. I also wrote to the recruiting oficers at Elkader, informing them that Nick was my man, and that I should have him. He started with us from West Union on Sunday; and when we arrived at Fayette we came across Minor Paign, a discharged member of our company, who persuaded Nick to sell him his cloths for $5. Soon the aforsaid Corporal arrived in hot pursuit. I told them that I should not give Nick up; but endeavored to satisfy them by procur-

ing the clothes for them; but Paign, true to the detestable reputation he has everywhere gained, would not rue the trade. They then determined to lay the matter before their commanding officer, Lieut. J.C. King, at Dubuque; and with this intention they went with us to Independence, where we stayed Monday night. Here we formed a strategem for outgeneraling the regulars, and making a good deal of fun. Having convinced the Dutchman that if the regulars got him to Dubuque, they would shoot him for desertion, and that there was but one way by which we could get him through safely, we gained his assent to our schemes; and with the aid of a citizen, we made during the night, a rough long box, and marked it "Hospital Supplies" &c. In the morning acording to Programme, Nick went to the regulars and told them he had concluded to desert from us and go with them; that immediately after breakfast he would go out of town and hide where he would remain until we should leave on the morning train; and that if they would wait for him with their buggy, he would return to the Hotel and go with them to Elkader. They believed him and waited. Immediately after breakfast he disappeared, went to the house where the box was; and there the boys nailed him up and put the box aboard the train. The plan worked finely until we got to Dubuque. It happened that the Corporal had written a letter to Lieut. King, putting him on his guard. This letter arrived at Dubuque on the same train which brought us. I left the box in charge of one of my boys, H. O. Bishop, who got it aboard a wagon to ship it over the river, while I went up to town to procure passes to St. Louis. The ice ran heavily in the river and the boat delayed about an hour before starting to go over, meanwhile Lieut. King had received the letter and was on the alert. Just as the boat was about to start, and while the boys were in the act of going aboard, he arrested the whole squad, expecting I was one of them, brought them back to the Peosta House and the box went over to Dunleith. When the teamster got over, he pitched the box from his wagon on end; and it so unfortunately happenend that the end in which the Dutchman's head lay, struck the ground, causing him no pleasurable sensations. He then leaned the box up against a building in such a position that Nick was compelled for a half an hour to stand on his head. When the cars had left Dunleith, a Dutchman came around, took the box down, and began to roll it over and over for the purpose of getting it into the freight house. Nick had shown himself capable of enduring almost any species of

80

torment; but the rolling process was too much for him. He called out in a sepulchral voice, for his tormentor to "quits dat." The Dutch railroad man, dropping the box, fled in dismay, swearing there was a ghost in it. Nick then entreated the bystanders to let him out. Some favored, some opposed. At last he knocked the end off and crawled out. When asked what he was doing in the box, he replied "peish co to var." Soon an officer of the law came across and told Nick to go with him. "I don't know about dis," said Nick. "Vot office you got?" The fellow replied that he was a Constable. Nick then said to him. "I let you know it take some higher Officer as Constable to rest me," The Constable then subsided and Nick went to a hotel. Soon some one telegraphed over to Lieut. King, and he came over and arrested Nick. The next morning he arrested me also, and released the squad. He took both of us to his office, and read certain "Articles of war" to us denouncing death &c for desertion and such offences, which caused Nick to turn exceedingly pale. I tole Lieut. King that I was aware such articles of war existed and that I intended to take his Corporal and Sergeant for violating them in persuading Nick to desert. He then agred to settle it if we would pay for the clothing, and expenses, which we did Nick having no right to sell them. Here the matter dropped. We held Nick....

Your Friend
DWIGHT.

In spite of diligent research on the part of the author, the identity of "Dwight" remains a mystery. Perhaps some reader will be able to verify who "Dwight" was, or if in fact this story is true

MARCHING ACROSS IOWA

Not all of the troops who enlisted during the war years of 1861-1865 fought rebel soldiers. Another aspect of the Civil War overshadowed by the larger involvement of troops fighting for the unity of our nation was that of soldiers sent west to protect settlements against the depredations and outrages of Indians such as the Sioux. These troops did not enjoy the lime light their comrades basked in as they battled the Confederate challenge, but their plight was equally as dramatic, often more severe, and just as colorful. Some Iowans, because of our state's proximity to the west, were sent to the western fronts. Among them were Henry J. Wieneke and Amos R. Cherry who had enlisted in the Iowa Fourteenth Infantry Regiment with Company B. Wieneke served as a cook, Cherry was Fifth Sergeant.

Companies A, B, and C of the Fourteenth Infantry were mustered into service at Iowa City on Oct. 23-25, 1861. They did not unite with the remainder of the regiment which mustered in at Davenport, and was ordered south. Instead, these three companies were ordered west to Fort Randall, Dakota Territory. On September 18, 1862 the three companies were withdrawn from the Fourteenth Infantry and formed into a battalion which was intended to be the nucleus of a new regiment, the Forty First Iowa Infantry. Later, even this organization was abandoned, and in April 1863 the Battalion became companies K, L, and M of the Seventh Iowa Cavalry which in 1864 participated in the campaign of General Sully against the Sioux Indians. Another Iowa Regiment, the Sixth Cavalry also served in the west. The words from Wieneke's diary, Cherry's reminisces, and a few other excerpts provide us with a view of the life, hardships and soldiering experiences of Iowans in the west. Unlike regiments dispatched to the south and east, they were given no transportation. Instead, they marched across Iowa, from Iowa City to Sioux City, to reach their destination.

Iowa 6th Cavalry headquarters in Dakota. The 6th and 7th Iowa Cavalries served in the campaign against the Sioux Indians out West during the Civil War. Both endured an agonizing march clear across Iowa in inclement weather to reach their destinations.
(Photo Courtesy State Hiatorical Society of Iowa— Iowa City)

Brigadier General Alfred Sully and staff. Sully conducted the campaigns against the Sioux Indians which the Iowa 6th and 7th Cavalries took part in during the Civil War.
(Photo Courtesy State Historical Society of Iowa— Iowa City)

* * * * *

....Our Battalion started from Iowa City on afternoon of Oct. 18th to march across State to Council Bluffs and up the Missouri Valley to Fort Randall Dakota.

Our rations consisted of Bacon Flour Rice Beans & Coffee. We marched all day & cooked near all night. We marched across the State to Council Bluffs weather getting cold and wintry and by the time of reaching Sioux City were facing Blizzards and below zero weather. Nov. 29 reached Vermillon the Capital of Dakota in Blizzard with heavy Snow 32 degrees below zero. Dec. 7th reached Fort Randall....

Here we spent wintr of 1861 and Summer of 1862 waiting orders to be relieved to go South. Instead on 1st of Dec. 1862 Co B recd ordrs to move to Ft Piere a Trading Post of the American Fir Co on west Bank of the Missouri River....Our march to the north was facing Snows and Blizzards for seven days. We marched through Snow Drifts with Thermometer below zero. When reaching Ft. Piere found quarters too small. The Company was divided 28 men with Capt Mahanna went to Fort La Fromboise a competing Fir Co where we camped.... In Spring of 1863 our Battallion was transferred to the 41st Iowa Infantry thus frustrating any hopes of being sent South. During the winter we rescued and sent South 76 white women and children that the Sioux had carried from Eastern Minnesota to the Missouri River.

Henry J. Wieneke

Note Wieneke's frustration, these soldiers wanted to fight rebel soldiers, not indians! Fort Randall was located about one hundred miles above Yankton South Dakota. Fort Piere was located at the junction of the Teton and Missouri River.

....We left Iowa City on the 31st of Oct and marched out two miles and went into camp at Gov Kirkwoods Farm and remained there in camp the next day the first of November Saturday Nov 2nd. Left camp Kirkwood at eleven Oclock A. M. and marched ten miles and encamped at or near the residence of Mrs. Douglass in Clear Creek Town Ship....

Sunday, 3rd. (Nov. 1861) Left camp again this morning at eight Oclock and marched twenty miles and encamped two miles east of

Marengo on Bear Creek. We marched very fast this day and was all very tired when we arrived in camp at night and you could have seen the men lying arround in all directions upon the grass or leaning upon their guns. The reason of their marching so fast this day was this. It was Co. C's turn to march to the right (or in front) and they made their braggs that they was going to run Co. A. and B. down before we reached demoin and they strung out like a pack of wild Bulls and at times they would call out to us (for we was next to them) close up Co. B. close up and we did close up to and tread their heels about as close as they cared abbout. We would have kept up with them if it had killed us all. Co. A. was in rear and would call out to give it to them Co. B. and I tell you the Wapseys as they call themselves got enough of that days march trying to run Co. A. and B....

Amos B. Cherry

Monday nov 4th 1861 Spent a miserable night verry strong fever, head felt like bursting. went into Ma(rengo) and bought Crackers &c and Carried crackers until dinner time when I caught up with the team we traveled 13 miles Encamped on mud Creeke.

Henry J. Wieneke

Monday, 4th. Left Camp this morning at eight Oclock and marched fifteen miles and encamped again on Bear Creek 12 miles west of Marrengo....On the night of the fourth we had a good supper in camp that we had begged allong the road and brought with us into camp. Our evenings meal that night consisted of Slap Jacks Molasses butter squash cabbage vinegar beef coffie shugar and milk which made up quite a styleish supper and you bet it was rellished by us all. After eating our evenings meal we all took to cuting up and having a good time in every way we could. Some was jumping others was wrestleing and others siting in their tents singing some favorite peice of music or an army song and another thing we had a fine lot of sport over and it was this. One of the men went out into the woods hunting and killed an Owl and brought it into camp with them. The boys thought this a fine chance to have some fun and at it they went. They would take the Owl and go slyly up to the dore of some tent and carefully draw open the folds of the tent dore and send the Owl in amongst the men that are gathered inside telling over the adventures of the day when in would come the old

Owl casting terror amongst the assembled Braves inside and the next thing you would see would be one of the boys running down through the camp as if all the rebbles of the south was after him and some ones head sticking out of the tent telling what he would do if ever he found out who done that and Lt. Schell amused himself by takeing his old Owl and throwing it into our tent and takeing me right fair in the mouth. No sooner had it come in than I went out and if I could have seen any one near I would have snatched him bald at one grab but the sport did not end here. He came into our tent after I had gone in and wanted to know what the trouble was (apearring very innocent). Says I you own up now to the truth or I will clean out every Lutennent in the camp and he roared out laughing which told us very well who done it. Well after awhile he went back to his tent and he and Lut Luse was studying over a pile of papers and in went the old Owl again right into the midst of the papers scattering them in all directions....
Amos B. Cherry

Tuesday 5th   Went ahead with team and Begged Bread had enough to feed them for dinner. Rested about 3 miles from Brooklyn   went in town and loafed until 4 oclock   camped north of town on big Bear Creek
Henry J. Wieneke

Tuesday, 5th. Left camp at Bear Creek at half past eight Oclock and made a march of twelve miles and reached Brooklyn at three Oclock, and camped near the town and near a creek of fine water....
Amos B. Cherry

Wednesday Nov 6th   Started at Six this morning and traveled 18 miles to grinel Powesheik Co   went ahead of the train and begged Bread enough for Supper   the Country this day was all prarie and you could travel for Hours without seeing a house. had another attack of fever this evening being the third   got medicine from the Surgeon   must Start at six tomorrow morning ahead of the train
Henry J. Wieneke

Wednesday, 6th. Left camp at Brooklyn this morning at seven Oclock and marched twenty miles and reached Grenell. We refused

to march in ranks to day on account of not getting enough to eat but we did not suffer you may bet for we called at allmost every house and in most cases found the people very liberal in giving provisions to the Soldiers....
         Amos B. Cherry

 Thursday Nov 7 Started in good time but on the wrong road and traveled 3 miles when I had to go overland or under land for it was all through sloughs for about 2 miles I traveled purety fast and made Newton by 2 oclock P.M. in the evening went up town with 200 wt (weight) of flour and took it around to different houses for baking. then unhitched on an open lot and went to sleep
 Friday Nov 8 Capt Mahanna arrived this morning at 5 oclock went around and gathered Bread got about 150 Lbs went down to Camp and went out on the State road Stopped at a farm house and Eat Dinner Went on made 20 miles this day the Sandiest road I ever saw Capt Mahanna gave me a letter from Carie this evening it did me more good than if someone had given me 50 D(ollars) am very tired this evening about 5 miles of the road was verry bad all sand the Horse Could hardly travel over it....
         Henry J. Wieneke

 Friday, 8th. Resumed our march this morning at nine Oclock and marched eighteen miles and encamped on Camp Creek fourteen miles east of De Moin.... I got the Boys together and out we went and paid our respects to an old Sescessionist that lived near by way of paying our respects to his hen roost and after getting a chicken or two apiece we returned to the camp and had a good mess of chickens that night and allso had the fun of stealing them besides....
         Amos B. Cherry

 Sat 9th 1861 Started ahead again and made 15 miles to Des Moines by 12 oclock had a hard snow Storm this morning but cleared up by noon Camped about half past 3 oclock in the forks of the Des moin and Skunk (sic. Raccoon) Rivers Des Moines is about 4/5 as large as Iowa City
 Sunday Nov 10th we did not move from here this day 1 man in Co C verry sick. not expected to live...
         Henry J. Wieneke

Monday, 11th. Still at De Moin. Today we performed the painfull duty of following one of our fellow Soldiers from Co. C. to the grave. His name was Maxwell and was from Wappello, Louisa Co., Iowa. He was burried with the honors of war. He was followed to the grave by the whole command in full uniform with unfixed Bayonets and arms reversed. The drums was all muffled which made them sound very solem indeed. We went from our camp to the hottell whare the Boddy was and formed in two ranks in front of the house. The Band then played one or two tunes and the Boddy was brought out before the coller company when the Band again played a very solem air. The corpse was then carried up to the right and the Guard arround it the Band in front. We was then brought to a right face and moved toward the grave yard which was about one mile distant. The Band played the dead march and nothing was heard but the solem sound of the muffled drums the steady step of the men and the subdued commands of the Officers. After we arrived at the grave we was drawn up in two ranks at the mouth of the grave and three discharges was fired over his grave and soon as it was filled up. After this cerimony we returned to town at a quick step the Band haveing taken off the muffles. They played Yankey Doodle, the Girl I left Behind me, and many other favorite airs. After we returned to camp and stacked our arms and looked arround the camp was still as a grave yard allmost not a loud voice was heard or any thing that would breake the silence and solomnity of the scene....
                                                                    Amos B. Cherry

The death was Wilson S. Maxwell of Wapello, in Louisa County.

Nov 12th 1861 Started at 9 Oc(lock) and traveled 14 miles and camped for the night Weather verry fine all day such weather is verry pleasant Camping out if it only stays so until we get to the fort I feel better this eve than I have since leaving the City
                                            Henry J. Wieneke

Wednesday, 13th. Resumed the march this morning at seven Oclock and marched twenty one miles and encamped on Coon River near the town of Reeding in Dallas County....
    Thursday, 14th. Resumed the march this morning at seven Oclock and marched thirty four miles and encamped on the open

Pararie near the town of Dalmanutha a small town of about one hundred inhabitants....After we had been there a short time and begun to talk about the war we found that we was talking to a lot of sescisionsts. They said it was good enough for us that we did not get enough to eat and that if we was fools enough to go to the war let us take what we could get. She said she had a son in the Iowa fourth Regt and he was a fool and hoped that he was getting the same fare as we was. This raised our dander a little and Trask told her about what he thought of her and the south. She said she would like to see all the oficers in the northern army hung. Says I you had better look out how you talk says I there is one of our Officers at the same time pointing toward Schell. She looked around at him and sneering said, Oh he is a little young thing I would not be afraid of him myself. This raised a perfect roar and neither took down the Lutenant....

                                              Amos B. Cherry

Friday Nov 15th Camp No. 12   Traveled 18 miles and Camped on creek a pleasant place the road this day was verry Rough up and down hill the boys went out this evening and found a Bee Tree and brought in about 40# of Honey Baked Bread until 12 oclock P.M. had a verry bad Head ache all day and still the toothache the weather purety cold this night. it friezes the Dough stiff for us. a hard life

                                            Henry J. Wieneke

Friday, 15th. Resumed our march this morning at eight Oclock and marched twenty miles and encamped on Turkey Creek in a fine boddy of timber....I started this morning with the front of the command and at night came in with the rear guard. I and Seargent Trask fell back on purpose. When we got back to whare the rear Guard was we found that they was about five miles behind the command and was driving three small hogs along with them that would weigh about 60 pounds apiece and was as fat as butter. I asked the corprall of the Guard what they was going to do with the hogs. Oh says he we are going to have some pork. Says Trask that is right we are in for that. O says some of the Boys you will report us. No says I wont do no such thing. I asked them if they was going to kill them. They said they was so when we got down in a hollow out of sight we loaded a gun and shot two of them and skinned them cut them up into small pieces and divided it arround amongst the six. Guards and Trask and I got all our Haversack could hold. We brought it into camp and I knew I was to be Seargant of the Guard that night and I told Trask that I would get the cook to cook ours after they had all gone to sleep so we hid it in our tent untill they had all gone to sleep and I took it out and the cook cooked it for me and I carried it and put it into the tent for Breakfast and you bet we had a good Breakfast of fresh Pork that morning besides giving the two cooks all they could eat. But our good fortune did not end here. Five of the boys were out in the woods hunting squirrels and came across a bee tree and about a barrell of honey in it....The next morning we all had honey to eat on our cakes which was a rare treat to me you had better believe.

Amos B. Cherry

Sat Nov 16th 1861   Camp No. 13   morning verry cold and windy   Started and went 17 miles   Camped 1 1/2 miles east of the village of Louis (sic. Lewis) on (Nishnabotna) Creek. commenced Sleating as we went into Camp   the tent wagon of Co C went ahead and it was 5 oclock when it Came back to Camp   we had hard times to Cook supper   The Slap Jacks were wet and like Dough no difference how long we baked them. this is a new side to Camp life, and a hard one. If we were only in the fort it would be all right then   everry tooth in my mouth is sore and aching and has been for a week or more. I went into a store in the town of Lewis this afternoon and it was so warm it made my head ache right away I could not stand it. did not wash the dishes this evening as it was so set. it is a little cold this evening but I do not feel it   I have got so much used to the Cold I do not think I could stand it in a house with a fire now   it would do as it did to me this evening in that store   Went to bed at 8 oclock this eve

Sunday Nov 17th 1861   got up at 2 Oclock and went to work. baked and cooked and started at Half past Sevon   the roads were bad being wet and frozen   went 25 miles this day and camped on the west side of (blank space) creek   the day was verry pleasant if the roads had only been good. expect to get into Council Bluffs tomorrow   I am very anxious to get there so that I can hear from home   I have been very homesick this day...

Henry J. Wieneke

Sabath, 17th. Resumed the march this morning at eight Oclock and marched twenty five miles and encamped on the west Nitchenie Bottomey the men very tired and lame and suffering greatly from sore feet I among the rest....While we was in camp at this place one of our commissary waggons caught fire and burned the cover all off of it and in trying to put it out the men distroyed about two hundred pounds of Flour. When the fire broke out about twelve Oclock at night the Guards gave the alarm and every one was calling out fire and of all the climbing I ever saw that beat all. Sometimes five or six would go out of a tent dore all at once and land in a pile at the out side for we all thought that the high grass had got on fire and was comming into our camp and we knew if this was the case our tents was a gonner for the grass was as high as my head and as dry as powder and our camp was in the midst of it. After the fire was put out it was fun to look at the men some of them had nothing but their shirts on some had their pants on and one Boot others had only their drawers. I tell you I had a good laugh over it to think how they got out of their tents. If the enimy had a come in at this time they would not have told us from a set of Indians....

Amos B. Cherry

Monday Nov 18th 1861 this morning was waked up by the Cry of fire fire The Co B Comissary Wagon is on fire why in the Hell don't you holler fire, and other such cries as the above one I was out of the wagon in less time than I ever went out before the wagon was all lit up I sprung for it and pulled up the cover then I pulled at the potato bag but it came out in pieces the Bean bag did the same flour Coffee, Beans potatoes and every thing else was mixed up we pulled out about 300# of flour 16# of Coffee 11 1/2 Bush potatoes peck of Beans and some other things we scouped them out on the ground and put out the fire when I happened to think that my feet burned and verry cold Started on and marched on 23 miles

Henry J. Wieneke

Monday, 18th. Resumed the march this morning at seven and a half Oclock and marched 25 miles and encamped on Mosquto Creek two miles from the bluffs. The men allmost gave out today....

Amos B. Cherry

Tuesday Nov 19th   went into town this morning and got a letter from my wife the child has been unwell the rest are all well   came back and brought 100 of Corn meal with me that I Bought there. about 3 oclock it turned up verry stormy   the wind viered around from South to northwest and it rained until about 8 oclock in the evining when it cleared up it is purety cold now

Wednesday Nov 20   Clear this morning but a little cold   got up at about half past 4 oclock and cooked breakfast   the day was verry pleasant. staid in camp all day   cooked dinner at half past 3 this evening...no news from home   am verry anxious to hear from home again how my Dear wife and children are   if I only had them near enough to see them once every day I would be satisfied but it cannot be. the men are all verry much dissatisfied with Pattee and getting more so all the time...

Henry J. Wieneke

Pattee is Captain John A. Pattee of Co. A, a native of Canada and resident of Iowa City. He was the Senior Captain, and in command of the men marching to Dakota.

Wednesday, 20th. Still in camp at the Bluffs. The men are threatening to stack arms if they are ordered to leave here without the asurance of being better provided for....

Thursday, 21st. Resumed the march to day at twelve Oclock and marched ten miles and encamped on Pigeon Creek ten miles north of Council Buffs and two miles north of Crescent City.... When we received the Order to march Co A and C struck their tents and made preparations to start but Co B was not to be decieved any further....we intended to obey all reasonable commands but we would not go any further without any thing to eat....we sat arround taking our ease not a tent moved not an article of Baggage toutched or a team hitched up and we was waiting to see how it would terminate. While we was thus waiting Capt Pattee came down with the extra teams loaded as had been said with eatables and Co. B. went to work with a right good will to striking their tents and loading their Baggage and took their arms from the stacks fell into line and reported themselves ready for duity....

Friday, 22nd. Resumed the march this morning at eight Oclock and marched twenty miles and encamped at Calhoun a small town in Harrison County. This day was very cold and windy. I and

Seargeant Trask fell back and took our time. The rear Guard over took us and we went on to gather for a mile or two and we concluded that we would disband the Guard and call and get our supper at some house along the road. So when we came to a house we all stoped ten of us and asked if we would get our supper. They said we could and set to work preparing it and a very good supper it was to....After we had finished eating we offered to pay for our meal but not one cent would they take. The old Grey hared man of the house said all he asked of us was to be good boys do our duity as soldiers and maintain the good name and honor of Iowa....

Saturday, 23rd. Resumed the march this morning at seven Oclock and marched fiften miles and encamped near the town of Little Sioux a small town situated on the Little Sioux river....

Sabath, 24th. Left camp at eight Oclock and marched eighteen miles and encamped two miles south of the town of Onowa a small town....

Monday Nov 25th Started at 7 Oc ahead of the train with Lieut Leuse and went on to Soux City 46 miles and got in the City at half past 7 oclock and stopped at the Heagy house got a good Supper I wish I could only get a letter from home then I would be all right.

Henry J. Wieneke

Monday, 25th. Resumed the march this morning at seven Oclock and marched twenty miles. We marched all the forenoon without seeing a single dwelling after leaving Onowa....

Amos B. Cherry

Tuesday Nov 26th 61 this morning it looked like rain and about 12 oclok it commenced by 3 PM the wind viered round to the northwest and began to get Cold men came in stragling by 3s or 4s at once this evening it is verry cold more so than any day since we started the old horse is not well had to trade off a pair of goggles to get him some medicine as I did not have a cent of money at five Oclock started with the team and flour and took it around to the different houses to have it baked

Wednesday Nov 27 the train Started at 11 A.M. leaving 1 team and several men at town myself amongst the rest to get what bread the women baked for us we waited until 3 Oc when we started...we went around and gathered Bread until 6 oclock when we started

out with about 600 lbs the teamster who was an Irishman got so drunk this afternoon that we left him in a Stable when we Started for the Bread and he only Caught up when we had started, still stupid we drove out on a verry rough raod over bluffs as rough as any we have been on yet-and got off of the road-when we were about 4 miles off from town and Sargent Trask and myself went ahead and hunted until we got to the ferry when we had to go back for the team headed by the ferryman and got into Camp at 9 oclock...
      Henry J. Wieneke

 Wednesday, 27th. Left Sioux City at eleven Oclock and marched five miles and crossed Sioux River on a ferry and encamped for the first time in Dakota....
      Amos B. Cherry

 Friday Nov 29th 61 this morning it is Clear but Cold the thermometer must be about 15 Deg below Zero we started and marched to Vermillion the Seat of Government of Dacotah Teritory here we had a verry good Camping ground with plenty of water I forgot to mention that last night we had to Carry all of Our water from one well half mile from Camp and had not enough to Cook Coffee...
 Sat Nov 30th 1861 Cold this morning but no wind looked as though it would rain also like snow marched 22 miles one man in our Company named Cannon an Irishman stopped at a house on the side of Gim river and Sold a blanket that he had stolen from one of his mess mates and traded it off for 1 qt whisky the officers sent a Corporal and 6 men back with him to the house and made him get the blanket and bring it home and then got a board & marked it with Chalk (stole a blanket and trade it off for whiskey) then parraded him through the whole Camp.
 Sunday Dec 1st Cold, Cold, verry Cold got up and started at Sevon Oclock the wind blowing sharp from north west traveled 17 miles the day was the Coldest we have had some of the Boys froze their fingers hands & ears. was sick with the Diarraeh had the home sickness more this day than any since we left the City...
 Tuesday Dec 3rd this the 4th anniversary of my Wedding opened up verry fine warm and pleasant as a morning in April Started and travelled 22 miles into the Indian reserve—2 miles back from our Camp we came across lodges of Indians in a Deep hollow. The Squaws & children Crawled through the grass looked like a flock of

quail   we did not get down to them as we wanted to get on and camp   our camp this evening is in a verry lovely spot the pleasantest since we have left the City it is on a flat (illegible) north east with the back toward a run on the opposite side of which were verry high Bluffs   covered with Cedar ash and Other kinds of trees the run was not frozen and the bottom pebbly I could have spent a week there verry pleasantly in such weather as we had

Wednesday Dec 4th   still verry pleasant and warm this morn Started at sunrise and made the station by noon 17 miles   the station as it is called is situated on the river Bottom and Consists of a large warehouse sawmill and lot of Indian Cabbins here you could see the natives in all states from those who were dressed in their skins to those who lived in houses and dressed better than I can here the Captain received orders to Cross the river and take up the west side but the teams would not do it as they feared that the Ice would break. I volunteered to cross with my horse & wagon and did so after I had crossed the Captain recd another order brought by an Indian from Pattee that we were to Keep on up this side for sevon miles further and then Cross so I had to go back   we then marched up 2 miles and camped on the Bottom   this evening our Camp was crowded with Indians until the guard had to drive them out...right of the post on the river Bottom & camped

Friday Dec 6th 61   this morning is verry nice again   Clear & warm this afternoon I went into the fort (Randall)   it is situated on a bottom   the Seccond Bottom from the River   on the west is a high bluff the fort is on as good ground as can be wished for   our quarters are good

Sat Dec 7th 1861   Started into the fort at 12 oclock   the Cooking Qrts are verry Dirty   made Dinner by 4:30   boys all verry well satisfied   recd 2 letters from home and am verry much relieved to hear that my family is all well...

Henry J. Wieneke

Excerpts from a letter signed W. A. M. which appeared in the IOWA CITY STATE PRESS on Jan. 22, 1862:

FORT RANDALL
DEC 28, 1861

....We arrived her about three weeks ago in good health and fine spirits. We had a pretty hard march of it, I tell you, but after all our trials, and troubles we have at last reached our destination, and found everything in much better order than we ewxpected....
....We have organized a debating society and have fine times. We also have a sabbath school and Good Templar's association. Capt. Mahanna is superintendent of the Sunday School. We also have a theatre once a month. There is a large theatre hall here large enough to seat four hundred persons; it is fitted up in style, with a splendid set of scenery. We have good times here if we are away out in the world, but it would be considerable better if there were about 500 girls here. They are a very scarce article about these diggings. There is any number of the true American ladies here but they don't exactly suit my style. There are about fifteen hundred of the red devils about the country here, and about two hundred hanging around the fort all the time. They are the dirtiest, laziest, lousiest, set of creatures I ever saw; I dont see how they live at all There is no game around here for them to kill. I believe they just live on what little they get around the fort.
W. A. M.

* * * * *

Excerpts from a letter signed A. R. C. (Amos R. Cherry), Fifth Sergeant of Co. B, in the IOWA CITY STATE PRESS, Feb. 19, 1862:

FORT RANDALL
FEB. 5, 1862

Mr. Editor: As I was a resident of Iowa City and acquainted with many in that place and vicinity, and was an occasional reader of your paper, perhaps a few lines from me would not be out of place, for the greater portion of our company is from Iowa City or from Johnson county....

....We arrived here on Dec. 5th, very much worn down by our long march; remained in camp two days outside the garrison to give the regulars time to get moved out of the quarters; took possession on the 7th; and we had almost forgotten how to keep house after living so long in tents. All the trouble we had was how to occupy all the room. Having been so long accustomed to sleeping four deep and mixing so thick in our six by seven mansions, it seemed very odd to us to spread out and live like white men once more. The quarters here are excellent, and provided with plenty to eat, which is cooked up in fine style by our friend, and accomodating cook, Julius Winekie. The members of Co. B are all well, not a man on the sick list from our company; and we are having very easy times during the cold weather. Since it became so severe, we have not drilled much; in fact not at all out of doors, but four hours each day in our rooms. Co. B is well drilled in the manual of arms, and I think not inferior to any company that ever left Iowa City for the war. We have been drilling some in the skirmish drill, since we came here. This is fine exercise and the men take interest in it, and of course learn very fast indeed.

And now a word concerning our officers. Capt. Mahanna is well and looks finely. He is the best captain ever had the command of a company of brave men; beloved by every man in his company....

Lieut. Luse is one of the best officers in the battalion, universally respected by the whole command....

Lieut Schell is young but an accomplished officer and brave soldier, and even to his seniors in rank, an example, and beloved by all.

We are in hopes of being removed from here and **sent South in** the spring to join our comrads in arms who are **with the devoted** and true of the Northwest....

A. R. C.

IOWANS OUT OF THE NORM

THE ARMY OF THE POTOMAC

A common misconception is that Iowans were involved only in the campaigns and battles associated with the south and the west. Though true of Iowa regiments, except for three that fought for a brief period with the Army of the Shenandoah during the Shenandoah Campaign from August to December 1864, there were Iowans who served in the renowned Army of the Potomac. Service in the south and west was no less heroic than service in the Army of the Potomac, but those who served in the Army of the Potomac definately received a higher compliment of glory and often better provisions.

The Army of the Potomac served in areas close to and around Washington D. C., and in Virginia, Pennsylvania and Maryland. This was an area of concentrated activity because of its proximity to the capitals of both the North and the South. Soldiers in this area participated in such renowned battles as Menasses (Bull Run) Gettysburg, Antietam and scores of others. It cannot be denied that the Army of the Potomac's service was meritorious, but being so close to the capitals of the North and South, military activity in these areas had the advantage of being close to scores of war correspondants whose dramatization of activities in these areas gained the Army of the Potomac more fame.

There were a few, perhaps one to two hundred that are known of, Iowans who served in the Army of the Potomac. Most who served in the Army of the Potomac entered through regiments of other states. Records of such entries are sketchy, and undoubtedly there are numerous examples yet, or maybe even never, to be uncovered. Known service in the Army of the Potomac through border states occurred in regiments of the 102 Illinois Infantry, 8th and 12th Illinois Cavalry, and the 2nd, 5th, 6th and 7th Wisconsin Regiments. In these, there were 12 men from Northeast Iowa who mustered into the Wisconsin regiments as early as May to August of 1861. Recorded enlistments of Iowa soldiers in other states regiments which served in the Army of the Potomac can also be found for a few individuals in the Third Maryland Infantry and Ninth New York Battery. Both of these, like the Illinois regiments, being later in the war. Soldiers who entered the service through these states probably had been recent relocators to the relatively new State of Iowa, and returned to serve in their native states.

One little known, but recorded, incidence of Iowa enlistment in the

Army of the Potomac occurred with a company of Cavalry in 1861. When the war machine was laboring to come up to speed, a local militia of cavalry from the Fort Dodge area whose inspiration for congealing was the Union loss at First Bull Run, found itself with no Iowa regiment to attach too. Hence, they traveled to Washington D.C. and became Company A of the 11th Pennsylvania Cavalry. Eighty three Iowans are recorded in the Iowa Adjutant Generals records as having composed Company A of the 11th Pennsylvania Cavalry. They were mustered into service on September 21, 1861 at Dubuque and left for Washington D.C. on October 6, arriving there on October 10. The company spent until November 17th in instruction and drill at Camp Palmer in Virginia. From there they marched to Annapolis and then to Camp Hamilton near Fortress Monroe where they spent the remainder of 1861 building quarters for themselves.

Some Iowans entered the Union Army as regulars. Records indicate that Iowans served during the Civil War in the 11th and 12th U.S. Infantry Regiments and the Second Regiment of U.S. Sharpshooters, all of which were detailed to the Army of the Potomac. Not noted in any published records is the service record of one individual who served most notably in the Army of the Potomac through the 2nd and 5th U.S. Cavalries and even participated in one of the first great battles of the war, First Menasses or Bull Run. This is the notable Thomas Drummond of Vinton, IA. Drummond was an emphatice abolitionist who had been Editor of the VINTON EAGLE, and both an Iowa State Representative and Senator. His patriotic committment was such that he did not wait for Iowa's mustering of troops. Instead, he enlisted within days of the Attack on Fort Sumpter in the 2nd U.S. Cavalry where he quickly gained the rank of First Lieutenant. The 2nd U. S. Cavalry later in 1861 became part of the organization of the 5th U. S. Cavalry. A war correspondence from Drummond printed in the Aug 1, 1861 edition of the VINTON EAGLE describes his involvement in the First Battle of Manasses. The battle occurred near Washington D.C., and was a confederate victory. Drummonds dates are in error, as the first Battle of Manasses occurred on July 21, 1861. His remarks in reference to the 18th concern skirmishing activities at Blackburn's Ford, McLean's Ford and Mitchell's Ford in Virginia.

From Lieut. Drummond

"I got into camp again yesterday. I was in the fight of the 18th at Bull's Run and the first shot fired by the enemy, (a rifled cannon shot) wounded the 2d Sergeant of my Company, (G) and wounded one other man and a horse. I had a private wounded afterward, by a Minie ball, while we were covering the retreat of the 12th N. Y. regiment, which broke and ran.

On Sunday morning at 2 A. M., I was in the saddle and never out of it except for a moment, until 9 A. M. of the 22d. We marched at 3 A. M. for our second fight, which proved to be the hardest battle ever fought on this Continent. We were defeated- routed-utterly routed and broken up. I was detailed at the beginning of the action to remain with my company (I command it) near Gen. McDowell, and had a full view of the whole battle, which lasted eight hours. Shot, shell, and Minnie balls rained around us, but the regulars stood like rocks. I lost four horses, but thank God, no men. When the retreat became a rout, I joined the remaining cavalry to protect the rear. After going 2 miles, I was detailed to the extreme rear, behind two of Arnold's guns. We went in sight of Centerville, when the enemy opened on our battery guns, and Col. Heintzelman under escort of my company, took the left, avoiding the road. I got into our old camp near Centerville, two hours after the other six companies of cavalry, and in two hours more again was in the saddle in full retreat through Fairfax. I did my duty, obeyed every order, was the last in retreat, [as I was at the fight of the 18th,] and yet was unhurt, not withstanding balls flew all about me. While acting as an aid to carry orders for the General, I kept thinking of God and Old Benton, trying to pray, and at the same time, keep the credit of Iowa good. It was a good joke on the praying I expect, but about the nerve and gallantry others can speak. I am not very brave you know, but pride will make even a coward stand."

Following Bull Run, Drummond was promoted to Second Lieutenant of the 2nd U. S. Cavalry. In the Oct. 23, 1861 VINTON EAGLE we find this mention of his promotion:

Hon. Thomas Drummond.

In looking over the list of Army appointments at Washington, we find that our fellow townsman, Thomas Drummond, has received the Second Lieutenancy in a Company of Dragoons in the regular army. We are rejoiced to know that Drummond has obtained a post at once so honorable, so agreeable to his feelings and so congenial to his tastes, for certain we are that he will discharge the duties of his new station to the credit of himself, and the satisfaction of those under his command.

We have known Tom for several years. First we knew him as a Land and Tax Agent, here in Vinton; next as School Fund Commissioner of Cerro Gordo County; next as an editor, associated with us in the proprietorship and management of the EAGLE establishment upwards of three years, during which time he was twice sent to the Iowa Legislature from this district—first as Republican representative and afterward as Senator.

We can say of a truth that his business tact and talent are clearly above the common average. In each of the positions above mentioned, he exhibited a sagacity and fitness which but few besides him possess. He was an excellent business man, a good legislator and a first class editor. With his fondness for the stir and bustle of active life, he cannot but be pleased with his present situation. He will without doubt make an efficient officer, and provided he survives the coming contest, will eventually make his mark as a military man, as we understand he has adopted that as his future profession. His numerous friends in this region feel a deep and uncommon interest in his welfare, and extend to him through the present medium, their best wishes for his unimpaired health, prolonged life, and final promotion to a sphere still more commensurate with his ability and manly ambition.

In this connection we have taken the liberty of copying a short extract from one of his letters to a prominent citizen of this town:

"Regards to all friends and assure the people of Vinton who have so honored me, that now I am called to another branch of the public service. It will be my constant effort to still deserve their good opinion. I have chosen a profession more dangerous than they gave me,

but one in which, in these perilous times, I hope to be not less servicable to the caue of freedom and constitutional liberty."

Drummond's service in the 2nd U.S. Cavalry ended on Dec. 31 when he recieve a commision to serve as Lieutenant Colonel of the newly formed Iowa 4th Cavalry regiment. It was not uncommon for such promotions to occur. Soldiers taking advantage of such transfers to volunteer regiments enjoyed leaps in rank and in salary!

Thomas Drummond from Vinton. State of Iowa Senator and Representative. Lieutenant 2nd U.S. Cavalry, Lt. Col. 4th Iowa Cavalry, Captain 5th U.S. Cavalry Company G.
(Photo Appeared in the July 1950 Issue of "ANNALS OF IOWA," State of Iowa Historical Society—Iowa City)

On The High Seas

As Iowans marched over the face of our nation fighting the land battles of the Civil War, some took to the water. Their service is less known as Iowa was not acknowledged in any way shape or form as a maritime state. As there was no naval recruiting station in Iowa, records of Iowans in the Navy are incomplete or poorly documented and credits were not given to the state for its young men serving in the Navy. In fact, service records of Iowans in the Navy are incomplete in the Iowa Adjutant General's records, and only four Iowans are mentioned as giving naval service in the extensive "Roster of Iowa Soldiers," There were, however, over 600 Iowans during the Civil War who departed from the standard Army enlistment and served on gunboats and other water craft of the

Navy. Iowans traveled to Chicago, St. Louis, or Cincinnati to enlist in their preferred branch of the service. Some even applied directly to naval vessels, and were from there taken aboard and duly shipped.

The Navy, just like the Army, had both regular and volunteer seaman. At the outbreak of the war, a handful of Iowans were serving in the regular Navy. Four; Lieutenant-Commander John G. Walker, Lieutenant George C. Remey, Lieutenant William R. Bridgeman and Ensign James Wallace distinguished themselves as line officers. James Wallace, on board the steam-frigate "Wabash," experienced warfare as early as August

27, 1861 when this vessel led an attack on Fort Hattaras and Clark in the Battle of Hattaras Inlet in North Carolina. The battle was a Union victory, the first major victory following the Union defeat at Bull Run, and a big morale booster for the Union. His vessel was also involved in the capture of Forts Walker and Beauregard on November 7, 1861, the same day Iowans under the direction of General U.S. Grant were involved in the engagement at Belmont in Missouri.

Iowans who held staff positions in the regular Navy at the beginning of the war were Paymaster's Elisha W. Dunn, and Henry R. Day, Assistant Paymaster John L. Woolson, and Edward B. Nealey who was Chief Clerk of the Bureau of Engineering.

In the volunteer Navy, Iowa made a credible showing in the number of seamen serving, and with 36 commissioned officers— all but nine of whom served in the Mississippi Squadron during the Civil War. The Mississippi Squadron was a fleet of seventy armed vessels. Iowa officers served on twenty-seven of them. Three of these officers attained the highest rank possible for volunteer seamen, that of Acting Volunteer Lieutenant. The value of this squadron to the outcome of the Civil War is best given by General Grant's statement in 1880: "Without them the Mississippi Valley could not have been taken by the army and held."

Also with representation from Iowa at the outbreak of the war was the Navy's land branch, the Marine Corps, In the Marines Iowa had four commissioned officers, one sergeant and five privates. The officers were; First Lieutenant James H. Grimes, Second Lieutenants William B. Remey Jr., David M. Sells, and William B. Murray.

Men who committed themselves to Naval service no doubt enjoyed not having to endure agonizing marches and other poor conditions experienced by the foot soldier. Their trade off, though, was for cramped quarters in poorly ventilated working conditions that were sometimes dismal at best, and in battle being sequestered to smoke filled stations below deck. That Iowa supplied nearly a regiment of seaman to the Navy without itself being a seaboard state, and without any active recruiting for the Navy is credible. It is testimony once again that Iowa's commitment to this great conflict, was sincere in every aspect, and beyond that for which credit is normally extended.

ORGANIZATION AND ELECTIONS

Military strength is quantified with various terms such as divisions, brigades, etc. Lewis F. Phillips from Gravity, IA., who served in the 2nd Iowa Battery, described the hierarchy of organization used during the civil war in his memoirs published in 1911:

> ....Batteries of field artillery were composed of six or four guns....When we took the field there were on the company rolls about 120 men, of whom were present for duty perhaps 90 men, with the three commissioned officers above referred too; about fifty eight horses, forty eight of which were in harness, the others ready to take the place of any that might become disabled in any way. A full regiment was composed of ten companies of 100 men each, commanded by a colonel, lieutenant colonel, major and adjutant. There was also with each regiment a surgeon with rank of major. These five officers were mounted; all others on foot. With each brigade there was always a battery of artillery. Brigades were composed of four or more regiments, sometimes commanded by a brigadier general, more often by the senior colonel of the brigade. Divisions were composed of two, three or more brigades, generally comanded by a brigadier general. Army corps were composed of three or four and sometimes more divisions, generally comanded by a major general. An army was any number of army corps that the President and the commanding general immediately under him might see fit to throw together, and received their commands directly from the President through the general commanding....A person not familiar with army discipline, on seeing an army in camp or on the march, might think it just happened so, but it does not just happen so. There is a directing force that controls it, and every man knows his place and is supposed to be there unless absent with leave....

Like artillery batteries, infantry regiments consisted, at full strength, of 10 companies. Each company averaged 100 men with 78 being the smallest allowed to make a company. Cavalry regiments at full strength were composed of 12 companies. The colonel, lieutenant colonel and major were commissioned officers of a regiment. Officers at the company level included captains, lieutenants, sergeants, and corporals. Company officer positions in the volunteer regiments were filled by election within the company. Individuals elected to these positions sometimes had prior military experience. Often the elected officers were successful businessmen, politicians, or otherwise prominent citizens, prior to the Civil War and their election was in no way associated with any military expertise. No doubt such elections were sometimes subject to the scrutiny of popularity and personal bias rather than true officership ability. Apparently the ability to read and write was, however, recognized as a factor in the promotional system. As stated by Colonel Noah Webster Mills of the Second Iowa Infantry Company D in a letter to his wife on October 9, 1862...."I have found in the army that the services of almost every soldier that could write were in demand...." Casualties were high during the war, hence leadership positions changed quickly, it not being uncommon for someone who entered as a private to be first or second lieutenant of their company within a few months.

John A. Mackley, of the Second Iowa Infantry Company A, described in his personal journal of the Civil War the first election of officers for his company, (then the Union Guards of Keokuk). Mackley fared well in the election, landing the position of Fourth Sergeant.

> *Apr 19 (1861)....Rices Hall Keokuk 7 Oclock P.M. Union Guards met persuant to adjournment J M Reid called the meeting to ordor & Capt Huston shortly made His appearance and took the Chair a committee was appointed to Keep out small boys*
>
> *J L Davis & C. E. Moses made patriotic calls for more Volunteers the Roll was passed around and several more signed. Three Cheers were given for Jas Cox a prominent Merchant of this City and a grey Headed Vetran who Came forward and Signed the Roll*
>
> *Moved Secconeded & Carried that we go into the Election of Officers*
>
> *Moved Secconeded & Carried that three Citizens be appointed tellers of the Election Chairman appointed C W Lowry, Capt Hagny & D A Thrall tellers*
>
> *Moved Secconeded & Carried that the room be Cleared of outsiders on accounte of Noise The Company then Marched out and made there first Perade on the streets for purpose of geting the Room cleared after Making a short perade on Main Street they Returned to the Hal*
>
> *On his own Motion Webster Balinger was permitted to Cast five votes in the election one for Himself and four as Proxy for the Absent Members from Sanduskey*

On Motion Doctor Bond took the Chair during the Election of Captain and Company then proceded to elect Officers
R. H. Huston & T. J. McKenney were nominated for Captain R. H. Huston recieved twenty four votes & T J. McKenney Recived Nineteen votes Chair declared Huston Elected and on Motion the Election was declared Unanimous Capt Huston Tendered the Company His thanks

On Motion T. J. McKenney was Elected first Lieutenant by Acclimation

S. M. Archer John Stannus and J M Reid were nominated for Seccond Lieutenant The Captain declared the firs Ballot illegal as there were too many Ballots Cast John Stannus Withdrew S M Archer Received twenty two votes & J M Reid Recived Twenty One votes Captain Huston declared S. M. Archer Elected Seccond Lieutenant

J M Reid was Elected third Lieutenant by Acclimation

J L Davis was Elected first Seargent by acclimation

Daniel Tisdale was Elected Seccond Seargeant by acclimation Webster Ballinger & John Mackley were Nominated for third Seargeants Ballinger Recived Thirty votes & Mackley Recived thirteen Votes Capt declared Ballinger to be duely Elected Third Sergt. Mackley was Elected fourth Seargeant by acclimation J C Wickersham was Elected fifth Seargeant by acclimation Thos Flood was Elected Ensign by Acclimation

S P Curtis was Elected first Corporal by Acclimation John Finnerty Henry Straus & R R Teller were Nominated for Seccond Corporal Straus withdrew Finnerty Received (18) Eighteen votes Teller Recd Thirteen Votes Capt declared John Finnerty Elected Seccond Corporal R R Teller was Elected Third Corporal by acclimation John Taugher was Elected fourth Corporal by acclimation....

Company adjourned....

May 4th State of Iowa Lee County May the 4th A D 1861 The following is the Oath administered to the Company by Oth Lyman Justice of the Peace

I do Solemnly Swear that I will bear true faith and allegiance to the United States of America and that I will Serve them Honestly & Faithfully against Enemies or opposers, Whomsoever and that I will Observe and Obey the Ordores of the President of the United States

and the Officers over Me according to the Rules and articles of War Further that I will Support the Constitution of the United States and faithfully demean Myself as a Volunteer and this Oath I take without Qualification or Mental reservation as witness my Hand
the Members Signed there names to the above Oath....

About this time we got a Blue Uniform from Vogel which cost thirteen Dollars each

Aboutt this time we also Elected four more Corporals as follows Eli Ramsey in place of Finnerty Resigned came in as fourth Corporal T A Stevenson as fifth Corporal G C Phillips as Sixth Corporal Wm Musser as Seventh Corporal Jos A Collins as Eighth Corporal about this time the Company Recd there Muskets & Blankets

INSIGNIA OF RANK IN THE ARMY OF THE UNITED STATES

Just as in today's military, the colors a Civil War soldier's uniform was trimmed with, and various other adornments right down to the arrangement of buttons, was a show of a soldiers' position in the chain of command. It was highly revered to wear the epaulettes and sabres of command in the days of the Civil War, where in spite of the wars bloody carnage, there still exhisted a robust air of chivalry between even the most hated enemy opponants. Following is an excerpt which appeared in the December 18, 1861 VINTON EAGLE Newspaper, explaining the adornments of Union officers uniforms:

The highest rank in our army is that of Lieutenant-General, and was conferred by Congress for merit on Winfield Scott, General-in-Chief, who is the only one who has ever held this rank in the United States.—The principal distinguishing marks of uniform are three stars on the shoulder strap or epaulette—a large one in the middle, flanked by two smaller ones—a double row of nine buttons on the coat disposed in threes, and buff sash, a straight sword, and a sword knot terminating in acorns. A Major-General is the same, but with only two stars on the shoulder. A Brigadier-General has one star, and the buttons on his coat number but eight in each row, disposed in twos.—The Colonel is the highest rank in a regiment, and wears an eagle on his strap, the buttons on his coat in double lines numbering eight at equal distances. When this officer is placed in charge of a Brigade he is called a Colonel commanding.

A Lieut.-Colonel is second in command of a Regiment, and is known by the leaf on his strap, which is silver, otherwise his uniform is the same as the Colonel's. The Major's is also the same, the leaf being gold. His duty is to act aid-de-camp of the Colonel, and in the event of his two superior officers being disabled or absent, he takes command of the Regiment; these three constitute the field officers of the Regiment, and are mounted. The Adjutant, whose position is the same to the Regiment as of Orderly-Sergeant to a company, and generally ranks as a Lieutenant.

Captains are commandants of companies, and are distinguished by two bars of gold on the shoulder strap, and eight buttons at regular distance in a single row on the coat; the 1st Lieutenant the same, but with one bar on the strap, the Second Lieutenant having a plain strap without marks. These last are called line officers; all Regimental officers wear a red sash.

The Surgeon ranks as First Lieutenant in the volunteer service, and as Major in the regulars, and has the letters M. S.—Medical Staff—embroidered on his strap, which otherwise is the same as a First Lieutenant; also wears a green sash. The Quarter master also takes a Lieutenants rank, and has the letters Q. D.—Quarter-Master's Department—and the Commissary with the letters C. D.—Commissary Department.

These constitute (with Chaplain, who wears no marks, only plain clothes of uniform cut) the Regimental staff, and are all allowed to have horses. The non-commissioned officers are Hospital Stewards, whose business it is to attend to the hospital stores and all the details of the Hospital Department, under the orders of the Surgeon.—His insignia is a green band on the upper arm, with a serpent entwined round a winged staff embroidered on it.

The Sergeant-Major is Second Sergeant in the regiment, and acts as assistant to the Adjutant. He wears a chevron (V) of three stripes, connected at the top by half circular continuations. The Quartermaster's business is the management of the details of that department; his chevron is straight across the top.

The Orderly Sergeant is first Sergeant in the company, and commands it in the absence of commissioned officers; the chevron is of three stripes, without connection at the top, and a diamond or star above. The Second Sergeant takes charge of half a company, called a platoon, and has the same chevron as the first, but without a diamond. The Corporals are in charge of sections or quarters of Company, and are distinguished by but two bars in the chevron. Of the sword the Cavalry saber is longest. The field officers come next; the scabbard being chocolate enamel, with gilt trimmings. The line officers, plainer and shorter, with sheath of black leather. A General officer's weapon is straight, with a guilt scabbord; Regimental staff is straight and short. Musicians, and non commissioned officers, being shorter still, more for show than use.

The color of the shoulder straps denotes the arm of the service—Infantry is blue; Artillery, red; Cavalry, orange; and rifles, green.

BACK HOME, ALL WAS NOT WELL

When husbands, fathers, and sons marched off to war, they left families behind, families that were dependent upon them as the bread winner and decision maker. Times were different then. Women did not enjoy the independence known to women of today and most were at home raising large families, some in homes no larger than a cabin and without all of the conveniences we enjoy today. When the husband left for the war, the burden of managing farms or other fatherly duties was left to the wife and children. Those left behind often suffered. The following correspondences between John Sharp, a private in the Second Iowa Infantry Company D, and his wife Helen Maria Sharp, describe how tough things got back home without the head of the household. The Sharps had settled near Kirkwood, a now abandoned post office in the northwestern part of Polk County. Mail service from and too the war fronts was slow, pay day for the soldiers was sporadic at best. Maria Sharp's chastisement of her husband for not writing often, or for not sending money reflects these problems.

* * * * *

December the 3rd 1861

Dear Companion....I am well and in good spirits. we had a pretty hard night the first night out. it was cold and we had 12 men in the coach. We got to st louis Sunday evening. we found 18 thousand men in the Bar (racks). there has been 4 thousand come in since. they had a grand Review Sunday evening and it was a pretty sight to see 20 thousand men on paraid and twenty full Bands playing. there is 3 regiments of cavalry and one of artillery. I have just come in from drill. there was a man killed Sunday evening by the accidental firing of a gun. it took the hole top of his head off. the health of the soldiers is good. I got a coat, pants and vest in Demoin and coat, pants and overcoat, two shirts, drawers and two pairs socks and shoes in St. louis so I have as many cloths as I can carry. I wish you had as many. I shall get my pay the first of January. then you can get some. I am not sorry I came. all that troubles me is you at home. I want you to get wilson and go and have that deed made out in your name. I will write you soon again and send you some stamps. I can not get them now....I would like to have your company but this is no place for you and my country calls me here. no more   from your ever true husband
　　　　　　　　　　　John Sharp

to H M Sharp

5th   I have just come in from Drill. I am well and getting along fine. we have plenty to eat and wear and we have any amount of soldiers here. we have 25 thousand. we drill twise a day and have dress paraid every evening. hartman is coming home in a few days. he is rejected. I want you to write soon direct Saint louis, Second Iowa Regiment, Capt. Mills, Co. D. Saint louis is a large city. I will try to send you some money by hartman. we expect to leave here in a few days for the south. we are going with the navy one hundred thousand strong with a hundred armed vessels. soldiers are coming in all the time. I think we will be redy to start by Monday. if we have good luck in clearing the Mississippi the war will soon be over and I think with the force here and on the river secession stands a poor sight. do the verry best you can and dont fret about me. I think it will not be long till the war will be over and I can come home and enjoy the pleasure of my family again. kiss those Dear children for me and tell them pa thinks of them while he is fighting for his country and for them. no more. My best love to you.

John Sharp
to his ever loving Wife H M Sharp

* * * * *

Dec 19th 1861

Dear John....we are all well in body but i cant say as much about my mind. i can hardly tell you how much trouble i see. you said before you went away that you would do all you could but your generosity overcomes your prudence so that now what my family will do for the winter is more than i can tell. your first payment has all gone but 4 or 5 dollars and i expect you will contrive some place for that. men say here that they will not give me one bushel of corn for that note and they say right out that (illegible) help your family for you (illegible) help so lazy a fellow as Joe Hartman. so you may be assured it makes me low spirited so that i cant help writing to you to not for gods sake if you want to save me from getting rid of myself lend your money till you relieve your family. i would not care if i had no children. they might get it all from you. now do not when you write again raise my hopes by saying you sent me the money. one happy night i thought by what your letter said that i would get it in the morning but it was missing and my disappointment is more than i can well bare. now do not raise any more false hopes for dissapointments nearly kill me. i cant eat nor sleep. my back hurts me so that i cant stand it to chop hardly at all. i shall have to brake up housekeeping before long. if i was only out of the way folks would take care of my children but to scatter them while im alive is more trouble that i can bare to think about. i got the letter that you wrote the 5th yesterday and had to pay 3 cents on it but he let it come out of the office. i want you to write once a week for a while and write more satisfactory. the children miss you very much but they will cry a while and then it is all bright again but with me i have only seen a few pleasant hours since you went away. that night that i got the letter and likeness before i knew that the money was lost i felt quite cheerful but it will not be long that i shall be troubled so i want you to keep out of bad company as much as possible. i know that it is difficult but you know you are not obliged to join them in there wickedness. i want you to be respectible if it is in your power. the baby has got so it plays a good deal and is going to be very forward. he can most sit alone. Allie wants you to come home and get your kisses. Ira cried the other morning for you to come home. it is very lonesome. i cant think of it with any degree of patience....i am so near wild now that one drop more trouble would upset my reason for i do not think that i am all right now. sis says that i am all the time muttering asleep or awake and i cant get hold of anything to do it right,. maybe you think this not a very good letter but i have only written the truth and put as good a face on it as possible. they came and got Jakes gun and ax and the rest of the things. i want you to write when you see Jake. i wrote for vine today. she got 11 dollars yesterday. i want you to send me some money as soon as you can but trust no one with it. the baby sis says she can pull hair and tell you that he would pull your whiskers now good. write soon and often. you dont know how anxious i am. this from your loving wife

      HM Sharp
my hair is come out till it is very thin. i am afrid i shall be bald.

January 14, 1862

Dear John....i have been quite well since i wrote before. i did not get any letter from you last week and felt very much disappointed and vine nor anyone got any. i begin to feel very uneasy. i wrote to you a week ago last friday and sent you bens letter and told you about what i got from the county and all the news that i knew. i want you to write oftener and tell us more news. you do not tell what you have to eat or how you sleep or anything about it. i have been gone from home since saturday. ....i waited till this evening to see if i would get a letter but as is my luck i am dissapointed. you write so little you will get out of practice and i shall feel as if i was neglected. vine got one from Jake. i heard that the boys all had the measles. why you dont write i see now. if you ever get uneasy about not getting letters you know something how i feel. the baby gros stedy and has great big blue eyes and a tooth most through. Ira says you must come home and i think you will have to manage him for he is most too much for me. allie says tell pa she has got a three cent piece that she is going to buy a letter with. now i shall have to quit for the want of ink. write soon....we most freeze chopping this morning. i guess i have frosted one of my feet some. you said that i would not have anything to see to but i tell you if i should wait to have someone come and see if i wanted anything i would both freeze and starve for no one comes in the house unless i go beg for it and sometimes not then. you wrote that you would send some more money the first of january but now the 16th and you have not even wrote in this month. i cant write any more for i have no more stamps or paper but write oftener or i shall give up all hopes. this from your wife

H M Sharp

you wanted me to make the children think you done right by going away but i cant teach them that when i know it is not right so i dont teach them anything.

THE FIRST DEATHS

The reality of war struck home when the first deaths occurred in a regiment. Many who wrote in their diaries and letters of the war, recorded their first experiences with death in the military, emotionally and vividly. As they went on in their service, many became hardened to the war's toll upon human lives, and paid death less regard in their writings. All who lost their lives in the cause of the war, however they lost their lives, are equally heroic. Yet, worth noting are the first deaths of Iowa soldiers in the Civil War.

Sketchy records early in the war create difficulty in ascertaining exact circumstances and events surrounding the first deaths of Iowans in the Civil War. The contention following the war, during construction of Iowa's Civil War Monument at the State Capital, was that seventeen year old Private Shelby Norman from Muscatine was Iowa's first war fatality. Norman was a member of Company A of the First Iowa Infantry (the first company to be enrolled in Iowa), and was allegedly killed in action at the Battle of Wilson's Creek on August 10, 1861. This thought prevailing at the time of the monuments construction, caused the commission overseeing the work to have the infantry soldiers likeness be that of Shelby Norman. A few notable facts surrounding Norman and his death are that it is believed his death may actually have occurred anywhere between August 2 and August 10 in skirmishing prior to and near the Battle of Wilson's Creek. No record was kept of the daily losses in these activities, the twelve casualties that did occur during this time period were simply lumped together in the category of "died at Wilson's Creek." It is also alleged that Norman was killed by a bullet that pierced his brain when he was marching to the Battle of Wilson's Creek from Springfield, a distance of 12 miles. Who fired the shot? Was it a rebel soldier or a misfire from a fellow soldiers musket? This fact is also unknown, but it does sound, from accounts, that it may well have been an enemy's bullet. Those near Norman when he was hit heard the dull thud of a bullet that found its victim, "The whistling bullet never heard by the one it hit, and which never hit the one who heard it."

The weathered face of Private Shelby Norman, 1st Iowa Infantry Company A, at the Iowa Civil War Memorial near the State Capital

There is ample evidence to suggest Norman was not the first to die in the line of duty from Iowa. The names of a few other individuals should be considered in this place of honor. For instance, there is First Lieutenant George Strong of Company E, Second Iowa Infantry, who was stricken with "brain fever" and died July 18. Strong, a 19 year old law student, was the first man from Jefferson County to enlist, and the first in the regiment to die.

A strong contention has historically been made for a private from Mahaska County as Iowa's first Civil War fatality. A plaque which once stood in the Oskaloosa, Iowa, city park, but now hangs in the Nelson Pioneer Farms Museum in Oskaloosa reads:

In Memory
Private Cyrus W. West
Company H, Third Regiment
Iowa Volunteer Infantry, Mahaska County
Killed July 11, 1861
In the Battle of Monroe Missouri
First Iowa Volunteer to Die in the
Civil War in Defense of the Union

There was no "Battle of Monroe Missouri," but there was skirmishing around Monroe, in which the Third Iowa Infantry participated. It is validated that this is when West died. He died from an accidental discharge of his own gun while he lay in a trench.

Casualties in the Civil War, be they at the hand of the enemy, accident or disease, were casualties all the same, and are treated so in military reports. Death by disease is a most unglamorous sacrifice, but the toll of disease accounted for sixty five percent of Iowa's casualties during the war. It is to disease that the true, actual, first death of an Iowan in the cause of the Union may indeed be attributed. Private Smith H. Tullis from Muscatine of Company C, First Iowa Regiment is listed as having died of pneumonia on or about July 3, 1861, at Keokuk, Iowa. Tullis was taken ill before the First Iowa moved south and was left behind. The MUSCATINE DAILY JOURNAL carried a report on July 5 that "Smith H. Tullis, a member of Company C, 1st Iowa Regiment, died of Typhoid fever in hospital at Keokuk, and his body was brought to this place on the Steamer Pomeroy yesterday."

Whatever the date of Shelby Norman's death, perhaps the one contention that cannot be disputed without the presence of more fact, is that he was the first Iowan killed from the first company raised of the First Iowa Regiment. And, Muscatine can definitely lay claim to the home of Iowa's first Civil War casualty, Smith H. Tullis. But the question of who was the actual first Iowan to die from receipt of an enemy's bullet may never be resolved until by chance some day a long forgotten correspondence or diary entry surfaces which gives testimony of some fact that it very well was Shelby Norman, or another of his comrades who were casualties in those few days before Wilson's Creek, or perhaps even some other heretofore unheralded incident.

The incident of what is alledged as Iowa's first field officer to die in service during the Civil War recieved considerable attention at the time, and appears well documented. Lieutenant Colonel August Wentz was a German immigrant who had served in the Mexican War. He came to Davenport in 1854, recruited a company of German soldiers and went into service with the Iowa First Infantry Regiment. Following expiration of the regiments 100 day term of service, he was given his commission as Lt. Col. of the Seventh Iowa Infantry by Governor Kirkwood. He was killed by a bullet to his side at the Battle of Belmont on November 7, 1861. An account of his death is provided by a sergeant of the Seventh Iowa in a correspondence to Brigadier General U.S. Grant:

BRIG. GEN. U. S. GRANT
Commanding District Southeast Missouri

My recollection of this officer covers but a short time. He was a German and universally beloved and admired. There was in camp at the time of the battle of Belmont a number of the wives of officers Col. Wentz among them. They saw their husbands off the evening before as they embarked on the steamers and turned their heads towards the enemy. The emotions of that hour who may tell?....

The morning of the battle as we had moved close up to the skirmish line and heard the brisk fire of the skirmishers and saw now and then one of them being brought to the rear all covered with blood it seemed a very trying moment. Col. Wentz came riding along slowly laughing and talking to the men and telling them how badly scared the enemy were thus breaking the force to the sickening sight. No doubt this helped many a poor fellow to stand up and do his duty creditably that day.

After going through the main battle and as the regiment was moving off the field and nearing the timber on the west, while I was momentarily back with Co. "B," Major, afterwards Gen. E. W. Rice, rode up and told us that Col. Wentz was wounded and had fallen from his horse then a little ways to the rear and ordered four of us to go back and bring him off the field; we went and found him, picked him up and carried him a ways until he requested us to lay him down. He felt he could go no further. We laid him down in the shelter of a large high stump. We ministered to him there as best we could giving him water and in trying to loosen his clothing could not get his sword belt undone and had to cut it to get it off.

As he could not bear to be carried further and was fast sinking a hurried consultation was held. We were in extreme danger of being captured as our forces had gone. The spot was swept by the batteries from Columbus and they were using them, several shots striking close to us and no telling how soon the infantry would be upon us. It was said he is good as dead and we had better save ourselves from being captured.

So two of the four started to catch the regiment and in a short time the third man thought it right for him to go too. I gave the Col.'s revolver to him and told him if possible to take that back to the Col.'s wife.

The end soon came as he sank rapidly. He had requested me to stay with him and now having done all I could I gathered up his sword and struck out after the command afoot and alone....Next morning reported my experience to company headquarters and turned over the sword to Mrs. Wentz....

I think it only a just portrayal of the temper of those times to state that when in a day or two, under a flag of truce, some of our army went back to bury the dead they found Col. Wentz. where we had laid him down but his body had been stripped of his clothing down to his underwear and everything of value on his person taken. It may be well for the coming generations to know that the pure hellishness of our enemies at that time seemed but one remove in atrocity above a blackfoot indian.

Respectfully submitted,
SERGT. J. C. PERCY,
Co. E, 7th Iowa Infty.

* * * * *

In Davenport, a patriotic funeral was given for Col. Wentz. In the procession were the Eleventh and Thirteenth Iowa Infantry Regiments, the Second Iowa Cavalry (these three regiments had not yet left camp), and many local political and community dignitaries. It is claimed his last words were "Let me alone boys; I want to die on the battlefield." His wife, who had accompanied him to the war front went on to the battlefield with other Union soldiers to find his body. Under a flag of truce, the battlefield on that day was occupied by Confederate and Union soldiers alike, both taking care of their dead and wounded. John Seaton,

Drawing of the 1st Iowa Infantry returning to Davenport following the regiments three month tour of duty.
(From the September 21, 1861 Issue of HARPERS WEEKLY.)

Captain of Company B, 22nd Illinois Infantry relates the following as he observed Mrs. Wentz discovery of her husbands Body:

"....*They relate some very affecting scenes they witnessed upon the battle-field, one of which was the finding of the body of Lieut. Col. Wentz by his wife. There lay the corpse on that blood-stained field, ghastly in the embrace of death. She stands gazing at it fixidly, and motionless as though rooted to the spot; presently her eyes fill with tears, and she breaks out in a low, agonizing cry: Poor—-poor—-soul—-is it gone? and falls prostrate upon his body. Then it was that stout and hard featured men wept. Every rebel officer took out his pocket handkerchief to wipe away the tears that came trickling down their cheeks. One of them remarked, `I'd give ten thousand dollars to recall that man to life'....*"

IOWA THREATENED!

Keokuk was an interesting place in Iowa during the Civil War. It was, it seems, a community focused on nothing but the war effort. Iowa's First Infantry Regiment rendezvoued and trained there and over the course of the war, Keokuk was host to four training camps and a large hospital for Union and Confederate soldiers injured in the Western campaigns. The city's location contributed to the fervor which prevailed in the community during the war. The Mississippi River was a thoroughfare for troops and supplies. Hence, Keokuk was the logical location for assembling and dispatching such elements of the war machine to destinations at the front. It was also the target for what could have been a fair sized engagement, maybe even a battle! A Confederate Officer, Martin Henry Green, who had recruited a cavalry regiment in Northeast Missouri, was plotting to get at ammunition stored in Keokuk. Union Colonel David Moore from Missouri was intent on stopping Green. Keokuk itself had amongst its population a contingent of people who were party to sessionist feelings. The whole situation created some dramatic times for Keokuk, Southeastern Iowa and Northeastern Missouri for a few months in 1861. Newspaper man C. P. Birge, writing in THE GATE CITY of Keokuk on April 22, 1900 captured the spirit of the area and the time with the following summary of the events reported in THE GATE CITY during April to August of 1861:

On the morning of April 15 news of Sumter first published.

April 19.—A meeting was called in Keokuk to consider the situation. At that meeting the late Justice Miller said, "Time for talking has passed, Time for action is here." A large number of distinguished and prominent citizens of Keokuk made speeches. Recruiting stations were opened for five or six military companies.

April 24.-The Keokuk artillery tendered its services to the governor.

April 25.-Public meeting was held at which W. W. Belknap offered resolutions that the duty of all was to "lay aside party affiliations and sustain the government regardless."

April 27.—Prominent editorial, Necessity of a Border Guard.

April 29.—Account given of the organizaion of the following military companies in Keokuk: The Union Guards, Apler's artillery, The Grays, Keokuk Home Guards, Rifle company, The

Jaegers, and we now find our first notice of a company called, "The Skirmishers," later the City Rifles.

May 3.—State authorities took possession of powder magazine at Davenport.

May 4.—Notice of organization of Cameron rifles.

May 7.—The Hawkeye State bringing three companies first infantry from the North. Powder house in Keokuk put under guard.

May 4.—Notice of organization of cavalry company; Torrence, Captain, afterwards Colonel Torrence.

May 11.—Notice of Union men being attacked by secessionists in Memphis, Scotland county, Missouri, and consequent exodus of a large number of families overland to Iowa along the border.

May 14.—First Iowa infantry mustered into United States service.

May 17.—Disruption of Cameron rifles, known as "Flitterfoots," and re-organized under name of Curtis Rifles, John W. Noble, first lieutenant.

May 18.—First public notice of City rifles. Call signed by R.F. Patterson, secretary.

May 22.—Captain Parrott's company took oath of allegiance.

May 25.—Picnic to regiments in camp. Address by Chief Justice Lowe to soldiers and General Samuel R. Curtis, Wm. Leighton, Samuel F. Miller and others.

June 5.—Captain Sample's cavalry company turned out thirty-two strong, and made a parade, being reviewed by Governor Kirkwood in a drenching rain.

June 11.—Public celebration of the funeral of Stephan A. Douglas. Both First, Second and Third Iowa regiments in procession. City rifles taking part.

June 12.—Flag presentation. Ladies of Keokuk to Union Guards.

June 14.—First and Second regiments left for Hannibal.

June 28.—City rifles, Captain Belknap and company, appeared in new uniforms. Navy blue shirts, gray pants with black stripe, cap of same color.

June 29.—Third regiment left for Missouri.

July 5.—Mention of City rifles performing everything in "Hardee" before a vast crowd. Complimented by Captain

Chambers, United States army mustering officer, and all taken to Young America for a treat.

July 10.—City Rifles elected Belknap Captain in place of Worthington who had been commissioned colonel of Fifth volunteers.

July 12.—News of organized rebels in Clark and adjoining counties. Threatening safety of Keokuk.

July 16.—News of expedition from Croton and Athens into Missouri to ascertain condition. Public meeting to organize citizens for safety.

July 18.—Public meeting slated by Captain Sample, General Reid, Samuel F. Miller. Committee of twenty-five appointed to take measures.

July 22.—Colonel Scott of Farmington took sixty muskets and ammunition for Farmington guards.

July 23.—Large number of secesh in possession of Memphis Mo. Much excitement in neighborhood of Athens(MO.).

July 24.—General Bussey reports distribution of a thousand guns between Farmington and Eddyville. Reports about 400 rebels within a mile or so of Memphis, Mo., generally disarming Union men wherever they can be found. Reports Colonel Moore with 300 troops about Athens waiting for more men. Much skirmishing in and around Clark county, Missouri.

July 25.—Keokuk cavalry elected officers. Torrence, captain; McQueen, first lieutenant; Reynolds, second lieutenant; D.A. Kerr, orderly.

July 26.—City rifles ordered in full uniform to escort Keokuk Cavalry company. Proclamation by Anna Wittenmyer.

July 27.—Presentation of flag by ladies to Captain Torrence and company Escorted by Keokuk Rifles, Captain Belknap, and Keokuk cavalry company, Captain Sample. Speech of presentation by Judge S. F. Miller. Famous response made eloguent by death of Captain Torrence, "We thank the ladies for this beautiful flag. Will defend it to the last. When this banner shall be trailed in the dust my wife will be a widow and my children orphans." All of which came true. A scene more patriotic and pathetic than any other in Keokuk duing the civil war.

August 3.—Fifth and Sixth regmients arriving, Colonels Worthington and McDowell. Expedition of Captain Sample's company in aid of Colonel Moore at Athens, leaving on special train at night. Camp in good order with about 400 men said to be not at all afraid.

August 6.—Account of great hurrying to and fro. Paper states rebel loss, killed and wounded, doubtless over twenty-five. Six or eight dead on the field. Rebels came in the afternoon under flag of truce stating they carried off fourteen dead. Many wounded and missing. Number estimated at 800 in the entire force. Names of thirteen union men wounded, and seven rebels. Paper states that 1,500 rebels were routed by only 500 men (at Athens, MO.).

August 7.—Account from Colonel Worthinton that his regiment marched some eight or nine miles to the rebel camp in the rear of Athens, but found that the rebels had not stopped under twenty or twenty-five miles. Worthington's troops staid out all night and then returned to Keokuk. Account of large number of volunteer companies from Primrose, Salem, Claygrove, and other points of rallying to the support of Athens.

August 8.—Report from Croton Colonel Moore with 400 men and six-pounder pursuing the enemy who had rallied to the number of 2,000 men, driving Moore back upon Athens. Special train will go to Croton. Great commotion. Citizens rallied in hot haste. Rifles and Rangers on hand in force. Several companies extemporized. Twelve-pounder taken to train. Vast crowd at the depot. Train departing with over 500 men. Banners flying, muskets gleaming, people cheering.

August 9.—Missouri rebel prisoners in court house. Mr. Timberman returned from Croton on hand-car. Colonel Worthington with five companies go out on morning train to reinforce Colonel Moore. Number of rebels killed on Monday now known to be forty-three and may have been more.

August 10.—Telegraph line completed to Keokuk.

August 12.—Prisoners released after taking oath of allegience. Word received from Colonel Moore that he had entered Memphis. Moore's forces now increased from 1,200 to 1,400 men. Headed for Edina, Knox county.

August 13.—Stampede from Canton. Greene's force threatening the town. Valuable service of Scott's Farmington company at Athens. Salvation of union camp at Croton caused by presence of Captain's Scott's Farmington Rangers, Keokuk City rifles, and Captain Sample's Rangers. Proclamation of Cyrus Bussey raising cavalry regiment for border service by order of Major General Fremont. Proclamation by Howard Tucker, orderly sergeant, City Rifles, calling in rifles, cartridges and cap boxes having been distributed to citizens on account of Battle of Athens.

August 14.—Notice of 350 to 400 troops marching from Davis and neighboring counties to support of Colonel Moore at Memphis. Colonel Moore sending his request for assistance to Captain Trimble and his company at Bloomfield. Captain Trimble proclaimed constitution and laws forbid citizens of Davis county marching to assistance of union men under Colonel Moore. Same idea of states rights that was debated at Croton as to policy of Iowa union soldiers crossing into Missouri.

August 15.—Paper states latest reports fix the number of dead picked up in cornfield and bushes. Rebel dead forty-five. Some citizens of Athens place it over fifty.

August 17.—Fight between Moore's forces and rebels about twenty miles west of Canton. Four graves on Fox river of noted parties said to have been killed at Battle of Athens.

August 20.—Colonel Moore in city holding conference with Colonel Bussey. Regiment arrived in Athens on the 18th. Company of Moore's went to Alexandria, Mo., arrested about thirty-two prisoners and brought them to Keokuk.

August 21.—Judge Rankin goes to Athens to act as judge advocate in examination of prisoners taken in Alexandria by Colonel Moore.

August 23.—Much renewed excitement at apprehensions of Tom Harris having designs on Moore and his camp at Athens. Harris reported to have 3,000 men with artillery. Colonel Bussey and local committee of safety took matter in hand to act with energy.

August 24.—Keokuk Rangers held meeting. Hugh W. Sample elected captain, Israel Anderson first lieutenant, John W. Noble second lieutenant, Wm. Wilson orderly.

August 26.— About 1,500 rebels reported between Athens and Edina. Moore to march directly for Kirksville with 1,000 men, fifty wagons and a brass nine-pounder from Keokuk. Parties wanting a taste of war recommended to join Moore. Sure of a fight if the enemy didn't run too fast. Prisoners taken by

Moore sent to St. Louis military prison by Judge Advocate Rankin and Colonel Bussey.

August 27.—Major McKee of Colonel Moore's regiment rode to Keokuk post haste. Large force of rebels were approaching Athens. Marching upon that place. At 7 o'clock fire bells rung, citizens gathered, guns distributed. Rifles and Rangers on hand. Nine-pounded loaded on train. Departed at 9 p.m. Another special left at 11 o'clock. Several hundred citizens landed in Croton soon after midnight. Rebels fail to materialize, being posted on reinforcements. Moore to march and hunt them, up whether or no.

August 28.—Reported that Green approached within eight miles of Athens on Sunday night. When being informed of heavy reinforcements abandoned the enterprise and retired.

August 29.—Reports that Moore has left Athens to join General Hurlbut at Kirksville.

REFERENCES

THE HAWKEYE STATE'S COMMITTMENT
Briggs, John E. "Enlistment of Iowa Troops During the Civil War." IOWA JOURNAL OF HISTORY AND POLITICS. State Historical Society of Iowa, Iowa City. July, 1917.
Gabbert, Dean. "First To The Front." THE IOWAN, Mid America Publishing Corp., Des Moines. June 1961.
Ingersoll, Lurton Dunham. Iowa and The Rebellion. Philadelphia: J.B Lippincott & Co., 1866.

IOWANS IN THE PRELUDE
Acton, Richard. "An Iowan's Death at Harpers Ferry." THE PALIMPEST. State Historical Society of Iowa, Iowa City. Winter 1989.
Acton, Richard. "The Story of Ann Raley: Mother of the Coppoc Boys." THE PALIMPEST. State Historical Society of Iowa, Iowa City. Spring 1991.
Graham, Paulene. "Springdale Recruits." THE PALIMPEST. State Historical Society of Iowa, Iowa City. November, 1928.
Graham, Paulene. "At Harpers Ferry." THE PALIMPEST. State Historical Society of Iowa, Iowa City. November, 1928.

LINCOLN'S IOWA TIES
Parish, John C. "Lincoln and the Bridge Case." THE PALIMPEST. State Historical Society of Iowa, Iowa City. May, 1922.
Petersen, William J. "Lincoln and Iowa." THE PALIMPEST. State Historical Society of Iowa, Iowa City. February, 1960.
Wilson, Ben Hur. "Lincoln at Burlington." THE PALIMPEST. State Historical Society of Iowa, Iowa City. October, 1943.

THE CHIEF CONFEDERATE IN IOWA
Mahan, Bruce E. Old Fort Crawford and the Frontier. The State Historical Society of Iowa, Iowa City. 1926.
Quaife, Milo M. "The Northwestern Career of Jefferson Davis." Transactions of the Illinois State Historical Society for the year 1923. Publication Number Thirty.

SOLDIERLY WRITINGS
Throne, Mildred. "The Civil War Diary of C. F. Boyd, Fifteenth Iowa Infantry." IOWA JOURNAL OF HISTORY. The State Historical Society of Iowa, Iowa City. January, 1952.

LOCAL COMPANIES FILL THE FIRST REGIMENTS
Briggs, John E. "Enlistment of Iowa Troops During the Civil War." IOWA JOURNAL OF HISTORY AND POLITICS. State Historical Society of Iowa, Iowa City. July, 1917.
"Iowa Cavalry." VINTON EAGLE Newspaper. Vinton, IA. June 21, 1861.

EQUIPPING IOWA'S RECRUITS
Upham, Cyril B. "Arms and Equipment for the Iowa Troops in the Civil War." IOWA JOURNAL OF HISTORY AND POLITICS. The State Historical Society of Iowa, Iowa City. January, 1918.

THE HAWKEYE STATE HELPED FOOT THE BILL
"Expenses of the First Iowa Regiment." VINTON EAGLE Newspaper. Vinton, IA. June 20, 1861.

THE CAVALRYMEN
Scott, Wm. Forse. The Story of a Cavalry Regiment: The Career of the Fourth Iowa Veteran Volunteers. New York: G.P. Putnam's Sons, 1893.

COUNSEL TO VOLUNTEERS.
"Counsel To Volunteers." VINTON EAGLE Newspaper. Vinton, IA. October 23, 1861.

ON THEIR WAY
Thomas, Benjamin F. "Off to the War." THE PALIMPEST. The State Historical Society of Iowa, Iowa City. June, 1941.
Throne, Mildred. "Erastus B. Soper's History of Company D, 12th Iowa Infantry, 1861-1866." IOWA JOURNAL OF HISTORY. The State Historical Society of Iowa, Iowa City. April, 1958.
Wright, Luella M. Adapted from a series of articles. THE PALIMPEST. The State Historical Society of Iowa, Iowa City. January, 1941.

IN CAMP
Ezell, John E. "Excerpts From The Civil War Diary Of Lieutenant Charles Alley, Company "C," Fifth Iowa Cavalry." IOWA JOURNAL OF HISTORY. The State Historical Society of Iowa, Iowa City. 1951.
Guyer, Hendricks. "The Journal and Letters of Corporal William O. Gulick" IOWA JOURNAL OF HISTORY AND POLITICS. The State Historical Society of Iowa, Iowa City. April, 1930.
Lucas, C.A. "A Soldiers Letters from the Field." IOWA HISTORICAL RECORD. The State Historical Society

of Iowa, Iowa City, 1902.

Mahon, John K. "The Civil War Letters Of Samuel Mahon, Seventh Iowa Infantry. IOWA JOURNAL OF HISTORY. The State Historical Society of Iowa, Iowa City July, 1953.

Martin, Richard. "Franc B. Wilkie—War Correspondent." THE PALIMPEST. The State Historical Society of Iowa, Iowa City. January, 1965.

Parkhurst, Clinton. "A Few Martial Memories: Off to the War." THE PALIMPEST The State Historical Society of Iowa, Iowa City. October, 1920.

Swisher, J. A. "Camp Life in Other Days." THE PALIMPEST. The State Historical Society of Iowa, Iowa City. October, 1941.

Thomas, Benjamin F. "Off to the War." THE PALIMPEST. The State Historical Society of Iowa, Iowa City. June, 1941.

Throne, Mildred. "Reminisces of Jacob C. Switzer." IOWA JOURNAL OF HISTORY. The State Historical Society of Iowa, Iowa City. October, 1957.

Throne, Mildred. "The Civil War Diary of C. F. Boyd, Fifteenth Iowa Infantry." IOWA JOURNAL OF HISTORY. The State Historical Society of Iowa, Iowa City January, 1952.

Wilson, Peter. "Peter Wilson In The Civil War." IOWA JOURNAL OF HISTORY AND POLITICS. The State Historical Society of Iowa, Iowa City. 1942.

MAINTAINING THE SUPPLY OF SOLDIERS

Briggs, John E. "Enlistment of Iowa Troops During the Civil War." IOWA JOURNAL OF HISTORY AND POLITICS. State Historical Society of Iowa, Iowa City. July, 1917.

Shilton, L. W. Unpublished letter from 14th Iowa, Co. I, June 23, 1863. Mt. Pleasant Public Library, Mt. Pleasant, IA.

A RECRUITMENT STORY

"Army Correspondence." THE PIONEER Newspaper. West Union, IA. Undated. Found in file AA2 at Iowa State Historical Society, Iowa City.

MARCHING ACROSS IOWA

Throne, Mildred. "Iowa Troops in Dakota Territory, 1861-1864. Based on the Diaries and Letters of Henry J. Wieneke." IOWA JOURNAL OF HISTORY. State Historical Society of Iowa, Iowa City. April, 1959.

"Iowa Troops In The Sully Campaigns," IOWA JOURNAL OF HISTORY AND POLITICS. State Historical Society of Iowa, Iowa City. 1922.

IOWANS OUT OF THE NORM

Dyer, Frederick H. A Compendium of the War of the Rebellion. New York: 1959.

Michael, W. H. "Iowa and the Navy During the War of the Rebellion." IOWA HISTORICAL RECORD. State Historical Society of Iowa, Iowa City. Vol. 10, 1894.

Roster and Record of Iowa Soldiers in the War of the Rebellion, Volume VI. Des Moines, IA. 1908.

"FROM LIEUT. DRUMMOND." VINTON EAGLE Newspaper. Vinton, IA. August 1, 1861.

"HON. THOMAS DRUMMOND." VINTON EAGLE Newspaper. Vinton, IA. October 23, 1861.

ORGANIZATION AND ELECTIONS

Phillips, Lewis F. "Some Things Our Boy Saw In The War." Self published recollections. Gravity, IA. 1911.

Throne, Mildred, "The Civil War Diary of John Mackley," IOWA JOURNAL OF HISTORY, The State Historical Society of Iowa, Iowa City. April, 1950.

INSIGNIA OF RANK IN THE ARMY OF THE UNITED STATES

"Insignia of Rank in the Army of the United States." VINTON EAGLE Newspaper. Vinton, IA.

BACK HOME, ALL WAS NOT WELL

Mills, George. "The Sharp Family Civil War Letters." ANNALS OF IOWA. State Historical Society of Iowa, Iowa City. January, 1959.

THE FIRST DEATHS

Sage, Leland M. "Iowa's First Fatal Casualty in the Civil War." THE PALIMPEST. State Historical Society of Iowa, Iowa City. November/December, 1977.

Smith, H. I. History of the Seventh Iowa Veteran Volunteer Infantry During the Civil War. Mason City, IA. 1903.

IOWA THREATENED

"WAR MEMORIES." THE GATE CITY Newspaper, Keokuk, IA, April 22, 1900.